YOUNG

YOUNG
IRELANDERS

Edited by
Dave Lordan

NEW ISLAND

YOUNG IRELANDERS

First published in 2015
by New Island Books,
16 Priory Hall Office Park,
Stillorgan,
County Dublin,
Republic of Ireland.

www.newisland.ie

PRINT ISBN: 978-1-84840-441-0
EPUB ISBN: 978-1-84840-442-7
MOBI ISBN: 978-1-84840-443-4

Typeset by JVR Creative India
Cover design by Mariel Deegan
Printed by ScandBook AB, Sweden

New Island received financial assistance from The Arts Council (*An Chomhairle
Ealaíon*), 70 Merrion Square, Dublin 2, Ireland.

10 9 8 7 6 5 4 3 2 1

Contents

Dave Lordan

Dave Lordan is a writer, editor and creative writing workshop leader based in Dublin. He is the first writer to win Ireland's three national prizes for young poets: the Patrick Kavanagh Award in 2005, the Rupert and Eithne Strong Award in 2008, and the Ireland Chair of Poetry Bursary Award in 2011 for his collections *The Boy in The Ring* and *Invitation to a Sacrifice*, both published by Salmon Poetry. In 2010 Mary McEvoy starred in his debut play, *Jo Bangles*, at the Mill Theatre, directed by Caroline Fitzgerald. Wurm Press published his acclaimed alt.fiction debut, *First Book of Frags*, in 2013. Also in 2013, in association with RTÉ's *Arena* and New Island Books, he designed and led Ireland's first ever on-air creative writing course, New Planet Cabaret. *Lost Tribe of the Wicklow Mountains*, published in late 2014 by Salmon Poetry, is his newest collection of poetry. Lordan has performed his own work and led poetry and fiction workshops at numerous venues and festivals throughout Ireland, the UK, Europe and North America. He is a contributing editor and short fiction mentor for *The Stinging Fly* and he teaches contemporary poetry and critical theory on the MA in Poetry Studies at the Mater Dei Institute of DCU. He is the founding editor of the popular and iconoclastic website bogmanscannon.com and he tweets @BogmansCannon.

Introduction

'Drive your cart and your plow over the bones of the dead.'
— William Blake, *The Marriage of Heaven and Hell*, 7:2

There are, have been, and will be innumerable 'Irelands', far too may for one kind of vision, one kind of fiction, one anthology, no matter how wide-ranging, to encompass. What this anthology celebrates and highlights is the emergence in Ireland in recent years of a young and versatile literature open to multiple experiences and points-of-view, to techniques, experiences, and accents previously little heard of or long repressed and excluded — without claiming privileged institutional or cultural status for any.

Perhaps there are no more interesting or various 'Irelands' for literature to feed on today than there have been at any other time in our history. Certainly, Ireland was at least as intellectually cosmopolitan and internationalised in the 1790s, that wonderful revolutionary decade, as it is today, to mention only one example. However, I believe there are more talented writers, in short fiction especially, coming from a far wider range of places and perspectives, with more things to say and more ways of saying, than ever before.

I

Although there is no simple or direct relationship between the progress of a nation and the kind of fiction its writers produce, there is obviously some connection. Ireland in its twentieth- century incarnation was really a nation of a defeated and downtrodden majority, a post-colonial people whose utopian hopes had been dashed and whose pride had to be swallowed and kept down, with painful difficulty, for a very long time. It is no coincidence that we became in this period the best in the world at producing the fiction of grief and of mourning, whether it is the damnation of the dead and the undead that animates the angry, vengeance-seeking grief of Liam O'Flaherty, or the instinct to sanctify the fallen, the downtrodden and the doomed that moves us so often in the work of Des Hogan, John McGahern, Mary Costello, Claire Keegan, Edna O'Brien and William Trevor, to name but a few.

The near unanimity of this variously shaded style of melancholy naturalism, despite the vast talents of its finest exponents, also quite clearly testifies to the monoculturalism that afflicted the Republic of Ireland in the twentieth century, and tempts one to describe Irish fiction in this period as a provincial or regional literature rather than a truly national one. A national literature that we can all feel part of, like that of the French, the Mexicans, or of the Egyptians, accommodates and encourages far more styles and approaches than Irish fiction has so far been generally able to, aside from the obvious exceptions. The most influential book in Irish twentieth-century fiction, it's ur-book and intertext-in- chief, is Joyce's *Dubliners*, a melancholy, naturalist classic for all times and all places. But Joyce, and after him Flann O'Brien and Beckett, wrote several other canonical works of fiction, whose influence on Irish fiction writers, in all but the rarest of cases, has yet to come to pass.

The diversity, alongside the success, of Irish short fiction in recent years gives grounds for being optimistic about the arrival of truly pluralistic and inclusive Irish literature in the near future, one in which no particular style or method is elevated to scriptural or exclusively state-subsidized status. There is unquestionably a new wave of young fictioneers emerging from our world-class small press and journal scene who are worth reading and supporting and who, between them, are building a sustainable audience for alternatives to the melancholy naturalist mode.

Some, but my no means all, of this new wave are represented in this *Young Irelanders* anthology, an anthology that makes no claims to totality or grand authority whatsoever. Think of it as primer, a mix-tape that will open your eyes and your soul to a new and continually evolving scene that is out there waiting to be discovered in literary magazines, small press collections, and in off-piste literary events of all sorts. You'll find your own favourites, I'm sure.

I am proud to present you with twelve new and diverse creations, from twelve new and diverse creators, with the *Young Irelanders* anthology.

My sincere thanks to all contributing writers, and also to the team at New Island Books.

— Dave Lordan

Kevin Curran

Kevin Curran's debut novel, *Beatsploitation*, was published in 2013 by Liberties Press. He was a winner of the inaugural Irish Writers' Centre Novel Fair. His work has previously appeared in *The Stinging Fly*. He has received an Arts Council of Ireland bursary for his second novel, *Citizens*, which will be published in 2016.

Saving Tanya

I only got on his Facebook once. He would always log out, but one day, yeah, he closed over the laptop when Mam came up and asked him for help with something, cos he always helped Mam with everything, and when I opened it, like, he was still logged in. I was gonna frape him, send loads of PMs to all the girls and put up a status like, I dunno, *I love dick*, or *Wish I had a dick*, or *I just did a great shit*, but then, like, then I saw the private messages he'd been sent, and I felt really bad for him, angry too, yeah, cos I knew some of the lads messaging him, and they always smiled at me or Mam, or patted my shoulder and said things like, 'Sam, the main man, how's your bro?' And then the messages they'd sent Jordan were cat. There was loads of them: *U Black Cunt* and *Can u hear me? Can u hear me? No. One. Likes. U.*

When he'd be taking me to town or to Deli Burger or GameStop I used be all proud and happy, cos Jordan, when he walked with you, yeah, he made you feel like a boss. Him and his magic aftershave would make all the girls from school call over and say hello. Even the girls from my class who I wanted to be with who never even normally noticed me would come over. They'd, like, all smile, or wave big, stupid waves from across the street, and the bigger girls, the ones from his year, yeah, would rub my head like I was a stupid dog or something and say, 'Oh, Jordan, he's got your eyes. He's gonna be a heartbreaker too,' and they'd all giggle and bring their shoulders up to their ears or mess with their hair. Emmanuel said they just liked Jordan and me cos we're half-caste, and that if he was half-caste they'd all come over to him too. But he was just jealous cos he was bleaching and still no girls noticed him.

But, what is it, sometimes if we were at the bus stop, or like, walking with the girls cos they wouldn't leave us alone going to the shops, some of those lads whose faces I saw on the private messages on Facebook would walk by. Three or four of them, yeah, all bumping into each other, and they'd see us coming towards them, like, and bring their hands to their mouths like they was hiding their face, and they'd say things like, nigger, or deaf prick wanker. Cos they'd go past so quick, and their mouths would be covered, Jordan wouldn't catch what they'd say. But I would, and the girls would too, and I'd feel let down by Jordan, yeah, like, I dunno, disappointed, cos like, he wouldn't fight back. And the girls' smiles would, like, turn, as if they just got a Mega-Sour or something, and things would go weird. I know he couldn't hear them, but they still said it and got away with it. All. The. Time.

My mam went mad after he was found. He was only missing a day, cos, like, his friend Dave knew where to look. Anyways, my mam was screaming and shouting and groaning, and all the neighbours just stood around being real quiet, whispering how he looked so peaceful, like he was sleeping, but I knew, yeah, that that was bollix cos he never slept with his mouth closed cos he had problems with his nose and his breathing used always keep me awake, and I used throw things down at him or rock the bunk or just tell him to shut up.

Sometimes after, when all the neighbours were gone, she'd fall to the ground and groan like an angry dog, and me or Woody or my little sister would try and hug her or pick her up, but she'd throw her arms out and tell us to leave her be. Times like that, yeah, when she'd go into a little ball and cry and cry, I'd wish I could help her, but I'd just go upstairs and find a jumper Jordan put in the wash but Mam never washed, and I would bring it to bed with me and hide under the cover and put my face in it, yeah, like a mask, like, what is it, I knew, I knew if Jordan were still there Mam wouldn't be so sad, and the house wouldn't be in such a mess and my clothes wouldn't be stinking and I wouldn't be robbing Febreze from Spar to spray all over them, cos I knew I was starting to smell like shit.

I remember playing football with him, just the two of us, yeah. I asked and asked, and then he said, 'Just ten minutes cos I'm busy.' But he wasn't, cos he was doing nothing only watching *Jeremy Kyle*, even though, like, I saw the lads he hung around with go past the house. So, what is it, we went onto the green and he stood around with his phone looking bored, and even though it was roasting, yeah, he had his hat on, the woolly one he always had on cos it went over his ear and hid his hearing aid. Anyway, I was running towards him and doing my stepovers and sending him the wrong way, and what is it, like, it was class cos every time, yeah, I'd nick it past him, he'd smile and say, 'Again, again,' and make me go back and get ready, and then, what is it, I was running, dribbling up to him, and he musta got a message cos I heard it and he looked at his phone and then, like, I was about to do my first stepover cos I was, like, real close, but still far enough away, yeah, and he just jumped at me, two-footed, man! He hacked me out of it, and I screamed out in bits on the ground, and I was like, I was crying and all. I feel bad now cos I got thick and, what is it, I was holding my shin and it was stinging and cos Jordan had tackled me he was on the ground too, and his hat had come off and his hearing aid was hanging loose and I went, 'Hah, you deaf bastard, I'm telling Ma.' He looked at me all sad, disappointed kind of, like he was gonna cry, and like, what is it, Jordan, yeah, he never cried, ever. And when he looked behind him those lads were walking backwards away from us into the lane to Lidl, and their phones were out and pointing at us and they were laughing. I grabbed the ball and just left Jordan there and tried to run home, but my shin and ankle was killing me, and I already felt like, ye know, I felt real tight for shouting that at Jordan, and I didn't know if I was crying cos I was sore or cos I loved my older brother and shouldn't have done that, like, shout at him like that, especially in front of those lads. Jordan musta come straight home after me, cos when I went up to the Xbox I heard the front door close and I knew it was him.

What is it, I played GTA all day and then went to bed and had to ask Woody to give me a hoosh onto the bunk cos my shin and ankle was still in bits. I was asleep, like, I didn't even hear him come in, when Jordan whispered in my ear, yeah, he musta shook me or something, and he whispered, 'Sam, Sam, you awake? I'm sorry, Sam. I shouldn't have done that earlier. Those lads texted me and took the piss. It was bad out. I'm sorry.' And he shook my head, and it felt great again to be his friend, but I never said okay or thanks or sorry. And that makes me feel bad now cos it might've helped him.

The next morning I had loads of mails, yeah, cos, like, someone had tagged me in a video, and the whole school, for real, like, the whole town had Liked it or Commented on it. Tommo had put it up the night before with the tagline, something about *this deaf prick can't even kick a ball*, and it was the video of me doing the stepovers and Jordan breaking me up and me crying, and Jordan on the ground trying to put his hearing aid back and taking his hat and looking over to the camera and the lads in the lane. You could hear them saying all sorts of stuff about him and me. And, what is it, you could hear me shout, 'You deaf bastard, I'm telling Ma,' and I felt bad out.

It was a bit after the Facebook thing that we moved house. She never said, yeah, but I think Mam musta heard from someone about all the Facebook stuff, cos like, what is it, I wasn't friends with Jordan so I couldn't see his page, but like, sometimes if someone I was friends with commented on a post, like, even to tell those lads to leave it out, I'd see the stuff. Maybe I shudda told my mam earlier, but, like, what is it, I didn't know it was such a big deal, an' anyways, we moved town. But Facebook isn't a house or a street you can leave behind, it's this thing – not even a friend, cos it doesn't ever really be nice to you – that you can never leave behind. And everyone on it, all the bad people, no matter where you go, yeah, they follow you and like, be like, always whispering, even sometimes roaring in your ear, like they did for Jordan, with everyone else hearing it too, like, about how bad you are, and like, how bad your life is. And no matter what, even your new friends in your new town would see it and wonder do you deserve it.

The inquest thing was put off by a few months after Mam asked the judge guy to look at Jordan's phone cos the cops had restored the factory settings on it and some old messages had come up. The judge lad said, like, he was asking Facebook to look at Jordan's account and go through his friends' messages too, yeah, cos Mam had convinced him Facebook was to blame as well. And when they said they would look at it, that's when Mam banned us from Facebook forever. Ye can't, though, ban Facebook. That's bad out, like. It's always there, it's everywhere, and everyone lives on it, even if Mam says ye can't go on it. But, like, I felt bad when I did go on it. Eliza never did. And she, yeah, she always whispered, 'I'm telling Mam,' when she caught me on it. 'You know what Mam said,' Eliza would say. Yeah, Mam said it's Facebook's fault. But it's not. It was the text messages, and Mam still uses her phone.

A few months later, yeah, Mam had to go see the judge again and Auntie Nelly had to come to our house, what is it, cos Mam was all upset leading up to it, like crying and stuff. All. The. Time. And Mam was staying in her bedroom and not coming out in the morning, even when we were going to school or being up when we got home, yeah. Me, like, I'm okay, yeah, like if I got upset I'd go to bed and get Jordan's aftershave cos he had nearly a whole bottle left — my mam got it for him for his birthday — and I'd spray it, just a little, *tssss*, yeah, on my pillow, and then be okay again. You see, Auntie Nelly washed all his clothes and pillowcases and all that so I'd have to spray his spray. Eliza, though, what is it, she was in the box room on her own, and she was only in first year, yeah, and me and Woody were bigger and in our room, but she cried a lot and banged on Mam's door and sobbed she wanted to come in, but all you'd hear would be, 'Go away, Lizzie,' as if Mam was, like, under the covers or had her head in the pillow too. Sometimes, yeah, at night I'd think of all four of us awake, but quiet and crying all alone in our pillows, wishing so hard that Jordan was here, and I'd think if only we were all together. But I never did anything to make it happen.

An' anyways, Auntie Nelly came that week, and I heard her talking, yeah, in Mam's room, saying, 'You've got to get it together, Marie. Look at me, Marie. You've got to get it together. You're gonna lose them.' And, what is it, I wondered then had Nelly been talking to Fiona too, cos like, Fiona was a woman I'd met in school who wasn't a teacher cos all she did was smile and whisper and look at me like I was sick, and say, 'What did you have for breakfast, Sam?' and 'Did you wash your clothes yourself, Sam?' and, what is it, I was angry with myself, cos like, I forgot to spray the Febreze on my shirt and jumper in the morning and she musta smelt the bang off me and in that room, yeah, and with just me and Fiona and another lady, it was so quiet you could hear my belly, like, going mental.

Jordan's inquest thing was on Tuesday, yeah, and like, we all stayed at home to look after Mam on Monday, and, what is it, we didn't have to go in on Tuesday, and like, everyone, even Woody, was too upset to go to school on Wednesday and Thursday and Friday cos Jordan was all over the papers, and like, even though Mam said I shouldn't, I could see his profile from his page used all over Facebook, and like, what is it, people that didn't even know him were putting up stuff about him and everything, like, oh, *I miss you* and *RIP* and *Gone but not forgotten*. But none of them said any nice things to him, yeah, when like, he was alive. Neither did I, but, and that makes me sad. He was my brother, and we never said, like, things like I love you, or you're great, or I think you're cool. And now, yeah, now, I really wish I did, cos maybe if he heard me saying it instead of reading the shit up on Facebook 'bout him, yeah, he could still be here and Mam wouldn't be so sad and missing all the time and Woody wouldn't be pretending to be asleep and crying, and me, I wouldn't miss my brother so much and be trying to make his smell bring him back to imagine the feeling I felt, yeah, when I walked with him down the street.

I decided to get off Facebook after I read in the papers about the judge guy asking Facebook for the messages. I had to rob the papers, cos like, Mam wouldn't talk about it. It was like, Sunday, yeah, and I was looking on the Settings to try and close my account when a new story just came up, and it was a link, yeah, what is it, Tanya Guildea, yeah, from second year, was Tagged in it, and it had two or three thousand Likes and hundreds of Comments, and I thought, yeah, it was gonna be like Nathan's from fourth year when he was skateboarding. Cos Nathan's video, what is it, was him skateboarding, and he, like, he broke his leg in it doing a trick, and the bone came out, and the lad recording it puked all over him and it was dead funny and sick all at the same time, yeah, and that video got like, nearly seven thousand Likes and over a thousand Comments. Everyone was talking about it, and even my cousins in Luton saw it, and I told them I knew him and they thought it was class. You could see his shin bone, and it was white and pink, and the skin was all ripped and his face was all white in shock, and it was rotten but real funny.

So, what is it, when I saw Tanya Tagged in the video I didn't know it was her cos the picture before you pressed play was a blur, but then you could make out her hair. Tanya, yeah, she was mad, like, she had long blonde hair, and she did it up like those drug-dealer girls from Ireland in jail in Mexico or something, and like, what is it, she always had loads of make-up on and her hands always looked filthy, cos like, what is it, she put so much fake tan on too. If you sat near her or, like, me, yeah, I was thrown out of class once cos we were messing – not together – I didn't really know her that well, but what is it, Miss threw us both out, so like, what is it, if you were near her perfume you would choke or sneeze and her eyebrows looked like they were drawn on, yeah, with like, a black marker, and if you stared at her or even nearly said hello, cos like, her eyebrows made her look like she was either angry or asking you a question, she'd say, 'What the fuck you looking at, freak?' And me, yeah, I'd just shrug and say nothing and run cos she'd beat the shit out of you like she did Liam O'Connell cos his locker was on top of hers, and one day, what is it, he let his books drop on her head and she punched him in the balls.

I was on the laptop, an' anyways, and I clicked on it and it was shaky at the start but you could hear Tanya's voice and she sounded locked, and what is it, then the picture cleared up and it was daytime in a lane, yeah, and there was three lads all with cans in their hands, yeah, and smokes, and they were standing against the lane wall, yeah, and you could hear Tanya but you couldn't see her, yeah, and you could only see the three lads from their waist up, and then the camera, what is it, the camera, yeah, it moved back or zoomed back and you could see Tanya on her knees, and she was like quiet now, and she was like, ye know, eh, getting busy, like, it was mental, and then when she finished with one lad, yeah, she crawled a bit over, yeah, and she like, when she was crawling over, yeah, you could definitely see her face, and then she started on the other lad. It was proper mental, like something out've a porno. I didn't Comment on it or Like it, but I checked who did, and loads of people from school all did, yeah, and they were all calling her a slut and a slapper and a skag and a whore and a hooker. All of the words, over and over again, *SKAG! HOOKER! SLUT! SLAPPER!* Hundreds of them, thousands of them, and like, me, yeah, I felt bad for her, and afterwards just thought of Jordan, and I dunno, like, seeing that on Facebook made me depressed or something. I just went to bed, didn't even reply to the Snapchats from Emmanuel or David asking if I'd seen the video, cos like, what is it, I thought I'd only make it worse for her, even though she was already an eejit. And even if she was doing that stuff, she probably didn't know she was being recorded, and with the lads all cheering and laughing it made her look all alone. Like Jordan, really.

I made sure I went to school the next day, and it was crazy and everyone was talking about it, and Principal O'Reilly came round, and even he knew about it, and said, like, what is it, he said the cops were looking at it – the dirty bastards! – and we weren't allowed to share it or talk about it, or, what is it, even look at it, but Emmanuel had it on his iPhone and iPad and his laptop already. People were saying stuff, like she was drugged and abused and it was on porno websites and all, and Emma Byrne said that Chloe, who was Tanya's best mate, said that Tanya had tried to slit her wrists and that she was being watched by a doctor and her mam at home. When Emma told me that story, she stopped suddenly and went, 'Oh, I'm sorry, Sam, I forgot about your brother.' I smiled like she was being silly, and said, 'It's grand, don't worry, Emma, it's grand.'

But I didn't go to class after lunch. I said to Emma and Emmanuel I was going to the toilet, but, what is it, I left the school. I met a girl from my year on the way out the gate, and she looked at me weird, yeah, and she went, 'You okay, Sam? Something happen?' And I just laughed, like, and said, 'Nah, just hay fever, thanks, Lucy. I'm going home.'

I dunno, all the stuff about Tanya made me think more about Jordan and Facebook and how all the stuff on it must've been stuck in his mind when he cycled up the Balla Hill onto the old Gaelic pitch with the long grass and all the cow shit, and went up to the posts, yeah, and took out the rope they said he bought the week before in Harry's Hardware and tied it round the old rusty crossbar, and then used the bike, yeah, to like support himself before he went, and I suppose, what is it, it made me sad and angry to think of all the bad things they said about him being in his head then and seeing all the profile pictures of all the bastards that hated him in his head on his last seconds in the world as my big brother. It wasn't fair. It made me so sad thinking of him having so many bad messages he couldn't stand it any more. It really did.

So I didn't go home. I went up Chapel Gardens cos I remembered Emmanuel telling me Frank could see in her bedroom window from the tree at the back of his house. Frank's da's car was a silver Ford, and he was on the dole, and I knew I'd find her easy if I found the car in the drive next door.

I wasn't sure what I was doing was right, yeah, but then I put my nose under Jordan's scarf and smelt his smell, yeah, and it felt like the times I was sick and I had to sleep on the bottom bunk in case I had to, like, get sick in the basin, or like, I had the scuts and had to run to the jacks. Jordan would give out, just so I wouldn't think I could get the bottom bunk forever, but I knew he didn't mind, and he'd be looking down on me from the top bunk, yeah, making sure I was all right, yeah, and, what is it he'd be saying, 'You all right, Sam? Will I get Mam?' or, 'Do you wanna drink of water?' Cos he did, yeah, look after me, always. And so I decided to do what he did, and look after someone too.

A woman answered, who I knew must've been her ma cos she had the exact same Angry-Bird thick eyebrows, and she, like, she looked like she was gonna spit on me or something, and I didn't know what to say, and she went, 'What the fuck do you want?' And what is it, I just went, 'My brother isn't here any more cos of Facebook. I'm in Tanya's class, an' ... an' I just wanna talk to her.' The ma, it must've been the ma, let her eyebrows wrinkle up into one mad single thick mountain of anger, and she said, 'I heard of him. Fair enough. Five minutes. And if you take the piss I'll break your bollix.' And then she roared upstairs, 'Tanya, there's a little fella from yer school here wants talk to ye,' and she nodded for me to, like, go up the stairs, and what is it, I ran past the ma and went up, and Tanya met me at her bedroom door in a T-shirt and tracksuit bottoms and she had no bandages or nothing on her wrists and there was no marks or nothing.

She flaked out on her bed and didn't even bother looking at me, and just kept watching, what is it, the computer screen, and her face was all pale in the light and she had black bags under her eyes, and her hair was in a ponytail, and she, like, she looked totally different, yeah, like, kinda all right, and I said, 'I just called to see if you're okay.' She tutted and shook her head like I was being a dope, and all she said was, 'Close the door,' and I did, and I sat at the end of the bed, and she, like, she just kept her face in the laptop and her toes were manky, kinda dirty brown from the fake tan, and her nails were rotten. It was weird being in her room with all the teddies and the posters of Iggy Azalea cos, like, I didn't really know her, and the only other girl's room I'd been in before, yeah, was like my sister's. But, what is it, I remembered why I was there, an' anyways, and I said, 'I know what it's like when Facebook ruins your life. My brother, Jordan, he, eh, he got loads of bullying on it and he killed himself. But you, eh, you shouldn't.'

She looked at me with that angry eyebrows question, and I didn't know, like, what more to say, and then she looked at the door and her eyes went like slits and she like, she whispered, 'Get a life, Sam. Kill myself? You mad?' And she turned the laptop round to me and she was on Facebook, and she said, 'I'm after getting a thousand friend requests already. I'm a fuckin' celebrity.'

Roisín O'Donnell

Pushcart Prize-nominated writer Roisín O'Donnell grew up in Sheffield, with family roots in Derry. After graduating from Trinity College with a First Class Honours in English Studies, she travelled and taught abroad for several years, before returning to teach in Dublin. Her stories and poetry have been published in *Colony Journal*, *Popshot Magazine* and *Structo*. In 2014, Roisín's story, 'Under the Jasmine Tree', was Highly Commended in the Bath Short Story Award. She has been shortlisted for the Cúirt New Writing Prize and the Wasafiri New Writing Prize, and her story, 'Him', received an honorary mention in the Fish Flash Fiction Prize 2014. Her short stories have been anthologised in *Fugue: Contemporary Stories*, *The Bath Short Story Award Anthology* and *The Fish Anthology*. Further publications are forthcoming in *Unfettered* (Tiny Owl, Brisbane) and in *Unthology 7*. Roisín has recently completed a collection of short stories which explores multiculturalism, marginalisation, identity and belonging in contemporary Ireland.

How to Learn Irish in Seventeen Steps

Step 1: Receive a letter with a fish jumping through a turquoise box in one corner. Unfold heavy blue-lined paper, translate neat black font into Portuguese and laugh. *Condicional?* They have got to be kidding. *A Chara*, Ms Luana Paula de Silva, thank you for registering with the Irish Teaching Council. Your registration is: CONDITIONAL. Your conditions are as follows: Irish Language Requirement. Time allowed: THREE YEARS.

During the first two years, you should:

Give in and bring Séan to Caraguatatuba, deep in the green belt of the Mata Atlântica, where Speak-Easy English School is seeking two new teachers. Over the next eighteen months, Séan's pale cheeks will freckle into a blotchy tan, fine lines will branch around his pond-green eyes, and he'll wear his thinning brown hair in a sweaty ponytail against the heat. Sometimes, on chirruping cricket-loud nights, Séan will play his guitar to you down on the *praia*, where skeletons of tiny crabs litter the damp white sand.

Celebrate your twenty-eighth birthday with runny chocolate pizza, Brahma beer and shots of cachaça. Try to teach Séan some Portuguese (he will never progress beyond *obrigada* and *cerveja por favor*).

Spilt the seam of your white chiffon dress thirteen minutes before you walk up the aisle in São Paulo. Your mama will stitch you back together, and her darting needle will prick your nutmeg skin. At this moment, your honey-brown hair should be sculpted into coils, and your mama's hands will be like frantic sparrows fluttering around your waist. Close your eyes and kiss the tarnished silver amulet of the *sorte* necklace your papa gave you.

Pose for photos with your new Irish in-laws against a sky of postcard blue. Hand-feed Séan *coxinha* and *pão de queijo*. Laugh when he takes pictures of the oozing *misto-quente* and black-bean *feijoada*.

Wrap your thighs around your new husband in the bathroom of the flat where you grew up, the back of your head rubbing against the yellowing *fleur-de-lis* wallpaper. Float hand-in-hand through the spiked palm shade of Moema and along Avenida Paulista, lined by its collar of skyscrapers. Take selfies in Parque Iberapuera in front of the towering banyan trees, their hanging roots like dark-brown dreadlocks.

Hug your mama in the glass-walled departures lounge at Guarulhos Airport and feel as if you have stepped outside your body. Whisper, 'I'll be home soon,' into your mama's crimped black hair and inhale her lavender musk. Your head should be crowded with voices begging you to stay.

Don't sleep during the sixteen-hour flight back to Europe. While Séan snores with his head on your shoulder, stare out at the pulsing ice-blue lights on the wing. Imagine the path you are charting through the mess of Atlantic stars, which will make you feel lost in the snow globe of space.

Step 2: Watch swallows perform roller-coaster dips and dives across the pale June sky. You now have less than ten months in which to learn Irish. Post a cheque for two thousand euro to register for the *Scrúdú le hAghaidh Cáilíochta sa Ghaeilge*. Séan will ruffle your hair and say: 'Seriously, babe? You think you can learn Irish in ten months? That's insane!' Fold your arms. Think: how hard can this language be?

Click 'send' on your two hundred and fifty-sixth teaching application. Start each cover email 'Dear Sir/Madam, I am a fully qualified primary school teacher with five years' teaching experience.' Drive the dank maze of Dublin streets in your silver Micra, delivering your neatly folded CV into the hands of various school secretaries, none of whom will ever contact you. After you have driven in the wrong direction up a bus lane for the third time in a week, Séan will buy you a satnav. Path-Finder98: Find Your Way Always. He will kiss your forehead, his lips like wet moth wings. 'No more getting lost, babe, yeah?'

Dye your hair Caramel Blonde. Put on five pounds. Haul your end of the leather sofa sideways through the narrow hallway of a red-bricked terrace with a purple door. Tentacles of ivy should crawl over your pebble-dashed walls from Glasnevin Cemetery. To fill the blank page of another jobless day, take a walk from your new house to the graveyard. Circle-headed Celtic crosses will resemble rows of people watching an invisible opera. Black yew berries will bleed onto the gravel path, and the industrial growl of a lawnmower will drown out the silence. Try to whisper the Gaelic inscriptions to yourself and wonder what they mean. *Go dtaga do Ríocht. Go ndéantar do thoil. I bParthas na ngrást go rabhaimid.* The chop of a spade will startle you from your contemplation. Your stomach muscles will tauten at the sight of a gravedigger slicing into the daisy-strewn lawn. Kiss your *sorte* necklace and try not to remember the undertaker's black-gloved hands at your papa's funeral.

Love the way your husband wears his long hair in a batik bandanna and strides around your new home like Kurt Cobain storming across stage. Watch him drilling holes in the freshly painted magenta walls, polishing his Vespa in the driveway and perching on stacks of cardboard boxes in the sitting room, practising his guitar. Drag Gabriela to every gig performed by Séan's band, Rootless Drifters. Feel blessed to be privy to the secret vulnerabilities of this confident man, his bottle of anti-hair-loss shampoo packaged like a petrol can, and the greenish skull tattoo on his left bicep, which he regrets. Happiness will swell in your belly, leaving you freefalling in a sense of joyous disbelief.

Step 3: On an August morning, quiver with goosebumps as you smile for photos on the windswept North Wall Quay, outside the tilted glass cylinder of the Irish Convention Centre. 'Naturalisation' will sound like a process involving dairy products. Buy a red body-wrap dress for the Irish Citizenship Ceremony (the dress will be slightly too clingy, so you will spend much of the day holding your breath). After two hours of sitting and standing, dozens of sweaty handshakes, an oath of fidelity to the nation and a flimsy certificate in a plastic sleeve, you should drink five pints of Guinness in The Quays and ask your father-in-law to teach you Irish. He will rub his speckled head and say, 'Oh geez Luana ... I wouldn't be a great Irish speaker now, sorry.'

Tottering in your strappy silver heels, approach Séan's sister and ask her if she could help you learn Irish. She will shake her shaggy blonde fringe into her pinot grigio and say, 'Ach, Luana, pet, I'd love to help you but I wouldn't have a fuckin' notion about Irish.'

Undeterred, ask Séan to teach you. He will hoot, 'Are you serious? That's hilarious, babe. Sure my Gaelic's brutal. *Cáca.*

Milséan. Banana. That's all I'd remember. Fuck, it'd be nearly impossible for a ... for someone from a ....'

How do you say 'foreigner' in Irish?

On the opposite side of the River Liffey, queue with Gabriela outside the immigration office on Burgh Quay in the washed-out light of 6 a.m. You will have agreed to accompany your friend to renew her visa because she says her English is shit and she needs you to translate. Ask her, 'Gabi, how am I meant to learn Irish when hardly any Irish people can even speak it?'

Gabriela will exhale cigarette smoke, her nose-ring glittering. 'Languages are weird, Luana. You know Irish is partly derived from Sanskrit?' Gabriela studied linguistics in Rio de Janeiro, but here in Dublin she shovels French fries into cardboard boxes for the minimum wage. You know your friend too well to ask her how this happened.

Step 4: Receive a call from Scoil Mhuire National School at 8:45 on a September morning. 'Aisling Burke's waters are after breaking early,' a mewing voice will tell you, 'we've a nine-month maternity post. It's short notice, but if you could come in today…?'

You now have a job. And you have seven months left in which to learn Irish. Kid yourself that watching *Ros na Rún* whilst lounging on the bed nibbling popcorn counts as a learning exercise, when in fact you're just dozing and reading the English subtitles. Switch the language on your phone into Irish (this will piss you off after a few days; change it back). Dye your hair Temptress Amber. Sign up for Weekly Irish Conversation Exchange at O'Donoghue's Lounge, where a man with veiny cheeks and rheumy eyes will lead you away from the other Irish speakers for a 'beginner session' in a shadowy corner of the pub. He will lean close enough for you to smell his oniony breath, and his beer belly will brush your thigh as he asks '*Tá tú singil?*' Leave early, forgetting your umbrella. Hurry into a sheet of rain, which will close up behind you, like the beaded curtain on your mama's kitchen door.

Enrol in Irish For Beginners at the Scoil Ghaeilge on Dame Street. Classes should begin on an October evening sweet with the fragrance of rotting leaves. Most of your classmates will be Irish retirees in search of a new hobby. If they gawk at you and ask why the feck a Brazilian girl like you is learning Gaelic, explain that you are a primary teacher with a Masters in education from São Paulo University, you moved here to Ireland because you fell in love with an Irish man, and that you must learn Irish in order to teach at primary level. Notice your classmates' eyes glazing over (at this point you should probably stop speaking). Learn your first phrase in Irish, and enjoy the Gaelic words undulating on your tongue. *Tá tuirse orm*: the tiredness is on me.

Learn 'indigo' in Irish.

Learn 'five hundred and seventy-three' in Irish.

Learn 'broccoli' in Irish.

Realise that at this rate it will take several decades for you to reach the required level of Irish fluency. Purchase a copy of *Is Féidir Linn! Teach Yourself Gaelic*. Inspired by a blue-skied Sunday morning, buy some sheets of brightly coloured cardboard, cut them into uneven squares and write the Irish on one side, the English on the other. Man. *Fear.* Woman. *Bean.* Heart. *Croí.* Break. *Briste.*

How do you ask '*você me ama?*' in Irish?

Turn off the bedside lamp. Kiss Séan's neck and wriggle against him. When he doesn't react, consider flicking the light back on. Say nothing. Perhaps fears are like *fantasmas*; if you don't mention them, then they won't be real. Lie awake in Séan's arms until he rolls over to sleep with his back to you. How long is it since you really looked at each other? Since he really saw you? Feel as if you have woken up into a nightmare and that reality is somewhere ahead of you in your sleep.

Step 5: Tear open another envelope with your teeth, leaving lip-prints of Sherbet Promise lipstick on the blue-lined paper. *A Chara*, an Irish inspector will visit your classroom on 3 November at 11:20 to assess the first stage of the *Scrúdú le hAghaidh Cáilíochta sa Ghaeilge*. In order to fulfil this stage of the assessment, you must teach a lesson using ONLY IRISH. *Má úsáideann an t-iarrthóir aon Bhéarla, ní bheidh sé de chead ag an Scrúdaitheoir marc níos airde ná 2.5 as 6 a bhronnadh* (ANY use of English will cap your mark at 40 per cent).

Panic. With the help of Google Translate, write out your entire thirty-minute Irish lesson like a badly plotted film script.

Shake hands with a tall grey-haired man in a green reindeer jumper and mutter an embarrassed '*Dia duit, conas atá tú?*' You will not understand his reply. He will take out his black clipboard and sit at the back of your classroom, almost doubled over on one of the yellow-legged infant-sized chairs.

Take a deep breath and give a fumbling lesson on *an aimsir*, during which Fionn will decide to steal Nabil's Spider-Man pencil case. In retaliation, Nabil will trap Fionn's index finger between two desks. Meanwhile, Belal will take a pair of plastic-handled scissors and hack Hamza's fringe off, and Beatrice will tug on your skirt and wail, 'Teacher! Agnieszka she say some bad word for me in Polish!' Attempt to resolve these disputes without using a word of English. Orchestrate an impromptu game of *Céard atá sa Mhála?* Rally the children into a song about a duck up a tree, which has absolutely no connection to the lesson you are meant to be teaching. At this point, thirty-two sets of small eyes will be regarding you with quizzical expressions.

Switch back into English as soon as the inspector leaves. Remind your class to 'keep your hands and your feet and your unkind words to yourself.' Your control over the class of six-year-olds should now be slipping through your fingers like a fistful of sand. Feel miniscule as a *tartaruguinha* being swept across oceans by the tsunami of the children's noise.

Following this sharp peak in noise level, you should be summoned to an after-school meeting with Mrs O'Reilly. The principal will pour you a cup of milky tea, pat her mousy bob and fold her hands in the lap of her floral skirt. 'Ms Silva, tell me, how are you finding the class?' Her tapered smile will not reach her pencil-grey eyes.

Mumble, 'Okay ... not too bad I guess.'

Mrs O'Reilly will sip her tea, 'Look, Luana, we're here to help you, pet. I know how difficult it can be, but the noise from your class this afternoon was through the roof. Through. The. Roof.' Nod mutely, to which she will continue, 'Now, perhaps you just need more support? I've noticed your class has fewer Class Stars than any other class in Scoil Mhuire, Luana. It would be great to change this, wouldn't it?'

Smile and gulp your tea. Part your lips, but find no words emerging. Contemplate robbing some Class Stars off another class's display board.

Step 6: Call Séan to tell him about your inspection. If he doesn't answer, phone his bandmate John, who will tell you, 'Sorry Luana, umm ... there was no Dustless rehearsal this evening.'

Say, 'Oh yeah, of course. It's Tuesday. Silly me.' Hang up. Blood will pound in your ears for a few minutes, making you feel as if you have gone temporarily deaf.

Stand by the stove stirring black-bean rice. Later, you will hear Séan's metal-capped boots stomping up the stairs, and the discordant strum of him retuning his guitar. When he plods into the kitchen, ask, 'So how was the rehearsal tonight?'

He will tell you, 'It was grand, yeah.'

Feijoada should now be simmering in the pot, fogging up the dark window. The warm air should be heavy with moisture, as if you were trapped in the entrails of the Mata Atlântica rainforest. While he speaks to you, Séan's narrow eyes will flit between the bubbling beans and the pearly buttons of your blouse. Experience for the first time the sensation of missing someone when they are standing right in front of you.

Step 7: Dye your hair Cocoa Velvet. Make sure you wear the black silk dress with the low-cut neckline to the Rootless Drifters' Christmas gig at The Bleeding Rose. (Your husband will tut at your cleavage and will say, 'Fuck sake, Luana, do you have to be so … so … so Brazilian?') John will pat your back and ask, 'Luana! I heard you're learning Irish. That's unreal. How's it going?' Tell him that you are progressing excellently and are now borderline fluent. If Séan then strides over and introduces the new bass player, Áine, who is a fluent Irish speaker, you should avoid her chirpy questions and feign indigestion. Leave Séan at the gig and hail a taxi home.

Slam the front door shut, hurl your red handbag across the room and twist open your last bottle of cachaça. Gulp down a slug of the clear liquid, which scalds a trail from your oesophagus to the pit of your stomach. Try to drink yourself into a place beyond thinking.

Open your sticky eyes five hours later, your clammy cheek plastered to the leather sofa. Wipe the spidery trails of mascara gloop from your eyelashes, and realise that Séan has not come home. On your lawn, the potted Christmas tree should have blown over into a sparkling heap. Waking up will feel like a feat of extreme survival.

Butter your toast, and use the knife to slit open another letter, leaving slug-trails of marmalade on the envelope. '*A Chara*, as a result of your classroom inspection, you have passed the teaching aspect of the *Scrúdú le hAghaidh Cáilíochta sa Ghaeilge.* As the next step of your Irish Language Requirement, you must complete a residential study period in the Irish-speaking Gaeltacht.'

Google 'Gaeltacht courses for primary teachers.' Book to spend a week at Coláiste Loch Con Nualla in Connemara during February half-term break.

Step 8: Whisper a prayer to São Cristóvão as you scrape the snow from your windscreen. Séan will watch from the doorway while you cram the boot of your Micra. Pack the fluffy blue Foxford your mother-in-law gave you, an AA road map, a backpack bulging with woolly sweaters, *Is Féidir Linn*, a three-pack of notebooks, your green weatherproof coat, a Tupperware box of *pão de queijo* from Gabriela and your last packet of Fandangos crisps. He will fold his arms and mutter, 'Fuckin' ridiculous … how the hell d'ya think you're going to learn Irish, babe…? Waste of money … probably get lost anyway … stupid fuckin' idea.'

Click the boot shut and throw your arms around his neck. 'I'll miss you.'

He will pull away and mutter, 'For God's sake, Luana, mind out for black ice.' Notice the coldness of his ferret-like eyes, the fact that he's wearing a Rootless Drifters T-shirt embossed with a logo of his own face, and the girlishness of his hand with its long guitar-strumming nails. Wonder why you never heeded these things before. Love and hate morph with the suddenness of a São Paulo nightfall.

Programme your Path-Finder98 and head west on the M4, through the flat expanse of the midlands. Bypass Galway City and continue through the outlying towns of Moycullen and Oughterard. Turn off the main Clifden Road onto a narrow, winding track signposted 'The Gaeltacht'. Follow the road as it weaves and curves around every ditch in the bog, but do not pay too much attention to the road directions you were given by the secretary at Coláiste Loch Con Nualla. These directions will not take you anywhere near the place you are trying to reach.

After two hours driving in desperate circles around the wilds of County Galway, realise that your destination isn't even on the map. Disconnect your Path-Finder98 and shove it into the glove compartment. As daylight fades, get out of your car and slam the door. Your breath will fog in the freezing air. Shout at a few uninterested sheep. Sense the hostile glare of this grey-green land in which you will forever be a foreigner. Cover your face with your hands. Remember the country you left behind. Ilha de Anchieta, where big-eyed spider monkeys perform acrobatics in the palms. Waves crashing on the soft white sand of Caraguatatuba. Your mama's hands. All of this you abandoned for a love as fleeting as quickly browning açaí blossoms. Pick up a rock and sling it into the mutilated darkness of the bog.

Get back into your car. Your bluish hands will be shivering on the steering wheel. How do you say *'perdido'* in Irish? Kiss your *sorte* necklace. Do a U-turn and judder back up the potholed limestone track. A snow-blotched sheet of bog will stretch for miles before it creases around the edges of the Atlantic. Yellow gorse bushes will be bright splashes on the tawny landscape. Gnarled branches of hawthorn trees will lean sideways as if caught in a perpetual storm. Locate the whitewashed farmhouse just as darkness has begun to drape across the rugged shoulders of the Loch Con Nualla hills.

Step 9: You should be greeted by a small blonde woman in a leopard-print apron. 'Come on in, pet, I'm Mary, your *Bean an tí.* I'll not make you speak Irish now, not to worry. You're from Brazil? My son's over there travelling, so he is.'

Follow her into a furnace-warm kitchen and find ten pairs of primary-teacher eyes staring at you like rows of politely seated orcs. Listen to ten names. Forget all of them. Accept a cup of milky tea and a slice of buttered soda bread. Feel an avalanche of exhaustion bury you when the other students ask why a Brazilian girl like yourself is learning Irish. Tell them 'I don't know why I'm learning this stupid language at this stage.' Some of the women will titter, perhaps unsure whether you are joking or not. Stupid *vacas.* Curse at them in your head in your crudest São Paulo slang. Duck your head away from their curious glances and swill your lukewarm tea.

Leave the kitchen and tiptoe into the dormitory. Undress. Lie on your assigned bunk bed and peep out through a chink in the threadbare curtains. The moonlit loch will be windswept into a texture like ruffled velvet. Shiver uncontrollably, despite your thermal pyjamas, Wilderness Explorer sleeping bag and fluffy blue Foxford. Consider getting out of bed to put on your woolly hat and gloves, but become paralysed by the leaden inertia of dreams. Think of Seán. Imagine that your bed is a raft that has been cut adrift, and that you will float forever without reaching the shores of this night.

Step 10: Attend lessons in the sea-facing classroom of Coláiste Loch Con Nualla from nine to five each day, but do not expect to understand a word the teacher, Kathleen, says. A wild-haired woman from the Aran Islands with a hooked nose and drawn-on eyebrows, Kathleen will not write anything on the dusty pine-green board, but will sit in a creaking armchair and reel off Irish sentences like incantations. '*Déarfainn ... déarfá ... déarfadh sé/sí ... déarfaimis ... déarfadh sibh ... déarfaidís ....*' Try to make some notes, but find yourself unable to do this because you cannot spell anything in Irish. Sneak out your mobile under the desk and try to Google 'spelling patterns in Irish', but find that there is no internet signal in Loch Con Nualla. Tears should sting, making your eyeliner bleed.

While waves of Gaelic roll over your head, look out of the tall windows at the lunar landscape, across which dry-stone walls are slung like broken rosary beads. Study a century of black-and-white school photos patchworking the rough stone walls, and try to envisage what it would be like to grow up out here, so far from everywhere. Think about the phrase 'non-national', and imagine yourself as a seed lifting on a chaotic breeze and drifting away from your home place, never to return.

Crunch back up the frosty hill towards your *Bean an tí's* farmhouse. Stop at a rusty gate to feed tufts of long, wet grass to two earth-brown donkeys, their hairy lips tickling your palm. 'Gorgeous, aren't they?' A square-jawed woman with turf-brown curls will stop beside you, rolling up the sleeves of her peacock-blue coat. 'So, are ye in Ireland long?' she'll ask as she pats the smaller donkey's tufty black mane.

'Eight years, almost. I came here for one year to learn English, but you know ....'

'Met a fella was it? Always the way. I'm Caoimhe.'

'Luana.'

Walk together up the rest of the hill in comfortable silence, past where an old red fishing boat is marooned on a bed of heather.

In the kitchen, Mary will be serving dinner. Douse your tasteless breaded chicken and over-boiled carrots in salt and pepper whilst zoning in and out of the teachers' loud conversation. 'So, you're from Ballinasloe?' 'Do you know Deirdre Fallon, the sister of Padraic and Séamus ...?' 'When we were above, doing the Leaving ....' 'Tell me now, would they be related to the McFaddens from Oughterard ... used to go with my cousin's friend ...?'

Once they have all gone to bed, sit at the kitchen table and copy passages from *Is Féidir Linn* into your looping handwriting. The only sound should be the scratch of your biro nib, the fingernail-drum of sleet on the window and the gurgle of the kettle on the cherry-red Aga.

Like salt crystallising on summer-beach skin, or the solidifying whites of poached eggs on a Sunday morning, begin to find patterns emerging from the embryonic mess of the Irish language. Nod with satisfaction when Kathleen tells you that the answers you've given to the *Modh Coinníolach* questions are spot on. Start to formulate simple sentences in Irish, and whisper these to yourself. *Luana Paula is ainm dom. Táim naoi mbliana is fiche d'aois. Is as Brasaíl ó dhúchas mé, ach táim i mo chónaí i mBaile Átha Cliath anois.*

Step 11: On your final night in Loch Con Nualla, link your arm with Caoimhe's to steady yourselves along the frosty lane. Watch the two brown donkeys trot into the village past the fogged-up window of McDonagh's. Spot the same two weary-looking donkeys plodding back up the road by themselves two hours later, as if returning from a night on the tiles. Drink pints of Guinness until you lose count of them. Sip your first shot of Jameson's. Down your second shot.

Follow a trail of laughter up the country road into darkness so tangible it should have a texture, a smell, a taste. This is the first time in your life you have experienced the real Irish night, away from the murky dishwater of the city sky. Explain this to Caoimhe. She will nod sincerely, although you have been speaking in Portuguese for the last ten minutes. Crawl into your bunk bed just as a pale yolk of sun rises over Loch Con Nualla.

Hand Kathleen a cheque for €1,200 for your stay in the Gaeltacht, and wonder if you will have to sell half of your internal organs to pay for the luxury of learning this language. Swap numbers with Caoimhe, who will hug you and say, 'Good luck, missus. See you in the exam.'

Drive back up the winding road, and watch the Connemara hills retreating in your rear-view mirror until the imposing mountains are nothing more than purplish fingerprints smudged along the horizon. Follow the M4 back across the belly of Ireland, sketching a line from one coast to the other. Three hours

33

later, enter the grey outskirts of Dublin feeling as if you are resurfacing from the swamps of a hallucination.

Step 12: When you pull into your driveway, Séan will be leaning on his Vespa with his wispy hair veiling his eyes. Under his leather jacket he'll still be wearing the Rootless Drifters T-shirt with the logo of his face on it. As you approach you will notice the khaki backpack on the Vespa behind him. He will put a hand on your arm. 'Luana, I've been thinking. Fuck it, it's just … with the new tour coming up … I just need some time to ….'

Shake your head, 'No, no, no, no.' Step into his arms and bury your head against the shoulder of his jacket. His sandalwood aftershave will take you back to the night you met, when his first touch evoked a type of muscle-memory, as if your body already knew him from a previous life. You already had your flight to São Paulo booked, but your plans to leave Ireland dissolved the minute Séan first hugged you. You sensed your future dividing like the Parnaíba River Delta, splintering into different paths.

Séan will pull back, taking both your hands in his. 'Luana, please … it's just for a few weeks, just till I get my head around ….'

How do you say 'stop talking' in Irish?

There are no words you could possibly say to Séan, in English, Irish or Portuguese. Stand in the doorway and listen to his bike chortling down the cobbled pathway of the home you once loved. After the snarl of his Vespa has faded into a whisper, watch a fuzzy rainbow leak through a slate-grey sky. At this moment it should be sunny somewhere on the horizon, but it will start raining where you are.

Close the door. Draw your burgundy living-room curtains, which will dye the room blood-red. Sit cross-legged in the epicentre of a grief that is every human emotion distilled down to 100 per cent proof. If your mama calls you, do not answer your phone.

Step 13: Teach. Sometimes you will need the distraction provided by your class of infants far more than they need you. 'Teacher, he hit me!' 'Teacher, my nose is itchy!' 'Teacher, she won't be my friend!' Through the eyes of your assembled six-year-olds, see yourself not as a broken wanderer but as a Fixer of All Things. On yard duty, try to keep check on the dizzying rush of children, an enterprise as pointless as attempting to patrol a hurricane. Pupils will swerve around the yard, haphazardly bright in their winter coats, like escaped pieces of a Cubist painting. 'I speak Arabic.' Nabil will skip up to tell you, his black fringe mad in the wind. Ask him 'How do you say hello?' Repeat after him. 'You're not exactly saying it properly, teacher,' he will smile.

After a rainy playtime, a type of mass captivity-induced hysteria will ensue. The children carry a constricted energy: flushed cheeks, scrambling, elbow-butting, pencil-fighting. In the midst of this chaos, you should attempt to conduct the daily Irish lesson. *Gorm ... Dorcha ... Bándearg ... Buí....* Mrs O'Reilly will stick her mousy-brown bob around the door and say, 'Oh how lovely, Ms Silva. I didn't realise you were teaching them Portuguese.'

Step 14: Read the next letter without translating it. Swallow hard. *A Chara,* your final examinations for the *Scrúdú le hAghaidh Cáilíochta sa Ghaeilge* will take place on Tuesday April 7 between 9:00 and 13:00.

You now have fewer than six weeks left. You will lose your Teaching Council Registration if you do not pass. Panic. Sit at your dusty dining-room table surrounded by toppled-over towers of Irish flashcards, mugs of whitish congealing tea, biscuit wrappers and stacks of dog-eared Irish notes. Over the wall, graveyard daffodils should bop their heads in the March breeze. 'Why don't you just give up and get a different job?' Gabriela will say. 'You don't even like primary teaching, Luana. Why not just quit?' Shake your head. How do you say in Irish 'I cannot give up now'? Run your hands over your face. Grit your teeth. Open a new chapter of *Is Féidir Linn*.

Listen to Kathleen giving free Irish lessons on Skype. During these lessons, you should contemplate:

Smashing the screen of the laptop against the bedroom wall.

Calling Séan.

Returning to São Paulo, where at least you wouldn't have to learn Irish.

Do not attempt actually to learn Irish or to write essays in Irish. If, spurred by a blast of hormonal enthusiasm, you happen to write an essay in Irish and email it to Kathleen, she will reply within ten minutes telling you 'It's complete crap, Luana,' and she will scold you for using Google Translate. Embrace the art of cramming. Read group emails from Caoimhe and the other Loch Con Nualla students (they are now placing bets on which essay question will come up). With blind faith, rote-learn the essays Kathleen has emailed you. Pray to every deity you know that Kathleen's predicted essay questions will come up.

Google 'fastest way to learn a new language.' Find out that the human brain is most likely to recall the information it receives immediately before sleep. Keep your Irish flashcards and rote-learned essays on your bedside table, and study them until your eyelids droop. Sleep. In your dreams, Portuguese, Irish and English should now be merging into one language. Dream of seven skewered chicken hearts cooking in the *churrasco* flames. In this dream, you will be standing on the roof of your mama's building in Moema, and Séan will approach you from behind, pushing you close to the skyscraper's edge. Wake up alone in your double bed. Stare at the ceiling while you figure out which set of sounds to speak.

Step 15: Sit at desk number thirty-eight and stare at the exam booklet.

SCRÚDÚ LE hAGHAIDH CÁILÍOCHTA SA GHAEILGE –
PÁIPÉAR I – 100 MARC
Trí huaire an chloig don pháipéar seo (10.00 – 1.00).
Cúig cheist le freagairt, ceann amháin as gach Roinn.

Write 'Luana Paula de Silva O'Connor' into the empty box using a running-out blue biro, so that the last letters of your married name are carved into the crisp white sheet. Caoimhe, wearing a canary-yellow cardigan, will give you a fingers crossed from across the room.

Feel a lump like hot *pão de queijo* in your throat when you open the booklet and see Kathleen's chosen essay question on the first page. Grip your *sorte* necklace. Regurgitate Kathleen's entire essay by heart as best you can. Have a guess at some of the other questions. Resist the urge to pass comment when two Irish girls stroll out of the *Triail Chluastuisceana* saying, 'That was easy wasn't it?' Do not shout 'IT'S VERY BLOODY FUCKING EASY

IF YOU WERE BORN AND BRED IN IRELAND, ISN'T IT???!' Feel your cheeks flush. How do you say 'Dear God, please help me' in Irish?

In the *Scrúdú Béil*, listen to your Converse creak across the shadowy expanse of the exam room. Sit down at a mahogany table opposite two old men with greyish whiskers protruding from their noses. Watch them demonstrate with great pride the device they will use to record your speaking: a machine that seems to have been resurrected from the 1960s. Don't give in to the urge to laugh hysterically at this point (it's just the lack of sleep). Listen to the old men's questions, and answer in Irish as best you can. You should be half-aware that you are throwing in the odd word of Portuguese. Hope that they don't notice. *Luana Paula is ainm dom ... Chuaigh mé go dtí an Ghaeltacht ar feadh um semana. Bhí bean an tí an-deas. Bhí sí tipo agus flaithiúil.*

After the exams, traipse down the hill to The Winding Road with Caoimhe and the other teachers. Drink two pints of Guinness and feel the tiled floor of the smoking area become as unstable as a sheet of melting ice. By now your head should be throbbing, your body drained and limp as a fallen leaf.

Slightly tipsy, call Séan and invite him to the pub. When he arrives and hands you a bunch of pursed-lipped daffodils, avoid his eyes. Stand by his side, swaying slightly. If he stares at you and says, 'Luana, please ... can we at least talk ...?' shake your head. If he tries to kiss you under the glow of an outdoor heater, duck away.

Gabriela will then turn up, pinching your waist from behind. 'Luana! What's this text about leaving Ireland? You can't leave! What will I do if you leave?'

'You're leaving?' The amber orbs in Séan's pond-water eyes will blur. 'Fuck, Luana, don't tell me you're fuckin' leaving?' Before you can answer, he will hug you tightly. Clasped in the bony warmth of his arms, your cheek pressed against his skull tattoo, a familiar darkness will gather inside you. A grainy blackness like coffee granules filtered through the stuff of days, building up as toxic sediment in the pit of your stomach. Swallow hard as a gritty feeling rises in your mouth. Push away from Séan, run past Gabriela, scurry into the Ladies, lock a cubicle door behind you and throw up into a toilet bowl. Rip off a sheet of loo roll and wipe the trail of watery vomit from your chin. Run your hands through the undyed roots of your knotty hair. *Santa Maria Mãe de Deus.*

Duck between elbows and out of the pub before either Gabi or Séan has a chance to see you. Newly arrived swallows will be skydiving across the bright spring evening. Take a shortcut home through Glasnevin Cemetery. Kneel and trace one of the granite inscriptions with your finger. *I líonta Dé go dtugtar sinn.* May we be brought into God's nets. The circle-headed headstones will eye you with curiosity, and a rat will scurry across your path from under one of the yews. Jog home through the bitter yew-berried dusk, lock your purple door and throw yourself onto your squeaky leather sofa. Don't worry if you do not understand why you're crying at this moment; you're not meant to.

Step 16: Wait. From the window of a Boeing 747, watch Dublin retreat beneath a torn veil of clouds, until the houses of your adopted city are so small you could scoop them up and fit them into your pocket. Spend the Irish summer at home in São Paulo, where it is winter. Refuse to talk to your mama about what happened with Séan.

Shut your bedroom door and stay in your room watching reruns of *Esperança* and listening to old Djavan songs on YouTube. '*Mais fácil aprender japonês em braile ... do que você decidir se dá ou não ....*' By now, the switch in seasons will have given you a head-cold. Your mama will pour all of her concern for you into her *feijoada*, and the smoky black-bean taste will catch in your throat. Take the elevator up to the rooftop at dusk to see the skyscrapers lit up like lanterns. Watch the shifting geometry of the São Paulo skyline and wonder why your birth city no longer feels like home.

Little things should now irritate you about São Paulo: the morning smog that chokes the canyons of Moema, the gaudy bombardment of advertising on the privatised Globo TV channels and the power cuts that frequently blinker the city for whole afternoons. You've lost your taste for *pão de queijo*, and *coxinha* seems too salty. Spend hours wandering around the city alone, circling the glassy lake of Parque Iberapuera, on which languid black swans drift. Google 'resettling in home country after living abroad', but this search will only provide information for rehomed asylum seekers. Spot a Tourism Ireland advert on a flickering billboard in a shopping centre outside Santos: three freckled children grinning against a purple-hilled backdrop. Freeze at the top of an escalator, felled by sudden emotion.

July will slide into August, and your mama will stop asking you when you're returning to Ireland. Celebrate your thirtieth birthday with a surprise *churrasco* on the terrace. As the pale winter sun plunges behind the back of the skyscrapers, pour another cup of milky tea and retell your mama the story of how you attempted to learn Irish. Already your life in Ireland will feel like a dream recounted by somebody else. Draft five emails to Séan, and abandon all of them. How do you say 'I'm lost' in

Irish? How do you say 'I'm confused' in Irish? How do you say how you really feel in any language?

Step 17: Lock yourself in your mama's bathroom and scrutinise the creased white envelope in your hands. On the now-familiar logo, the Salmon of Knowledge will leap through a square of cobalt-blue. Lean your head against the sun-bleached wallpaper. Imagine the worn-out tendrils of the *fleur-de-lis* weaving into your honey-brown hair and rooting you to this place. Try to formulate a single sentence that will express the meaning of your eight years in Ireland. Close your eyes. Take a deep breath. Kiss your *sorte* necklace and wonder what your papa would make of all this. Rip open the envelope with shaking hands.

Fling the bathroom door open and shout out 'Mama, guess what!'

Rob Doyle

R ob Doyle's first novel, *Here Are the Young Men*, was published
in 2014 by Bloomsbury and the Lilliput Press. His second
book, *This Is the Ritual*, will be published in January 2016
(Bloomsbury / Lilliput). Rob's fiction, essays, and reviews have
appeared in *The Dublin Review, The Irish Times, The Sunday Times,
The Stinging Fly, The Sunday Business Post, gorse,* and elsewhere. Rob
studied Philosophy and Psychoanalysis at Trinity College,
Dublin.

Summer
(Trevor, Lena, Martin)

Men don't regret cheating actually, only the consequences. This is what I feel.

a moment of vertigo. (The bloody O of Paddy's mouth, rain of white glints in the gush.)

I rode your sister, he thought.

*

I wouldn't do it like that. You always have that power, that possibility with men. You can kill them if you want to.

*

He took me back to a party on a roof. It was in Kreuzberg, and mostly older people, in their thirties. It was a sunny morning again. We drank vodka and orange juice and ate some food. There was

43

a DJ up on the roof playing trance stuff, kind of ambient, really beautiful. The boy had more cocaine. I thought about Axel

*

the intention had been to sleep separately, but after a few glasses of wine on the Rue des Eperonniers

the balcony, fumbling the door handle. He clutched the rail and peered down over the Fairview Road. There was a white car, near the entrance

he cheated on me at a party when I was in Cologne to visit my sister. He kept saying he was really high when it happened, taking lots of drugs, and it was just pure fucking, no feeling. A dancing girl who was smiling at him. But this only made it worse

take some of his coke in a cubicle

It was so fucking cool. Every time a train was going over your head the whole club was shaking.

you came onto the train. It was as if you were him.

*

We bought some bottles and sat out in Treptower Park. There were lots of punks, anarchists, groups of people starting off their weekend.

all the bullshit in our relationship

Even in his red Nissan Almera he felt exposed, as if he were driving under a flashing neon arrow

the rooftop and the city. Traffic starting alive in the morning. To be young, she thought

I knew it was real

'He stabbed his friend to death. They were taking amphetamines.'

*

it was as if she was going along with the expectations imposed by waking up beside a man, while inwardly sceptical of the encounter.

she was young

*

A bell rang in a distant church tower. Something spooked the pigeons and they rose, flapping

Standing by the coastal wall, he flung the butt of his cigarette into the rocks. He called Lucy. 'I need to borrow a sleeping bag,' he said. 'I need it tonight.' He put his hand against the car. He thought he would vomit.

Karen was close to the wall, facing it.

This is what I feel.

✢

I stayed in the park, watching people, sending texts. Thinking of Axel. There was no point going home.

he abandoned the car in a cul de sac off the North Circular Road.

There was a man sitting alone at a table next to Martin. He looked right ahead, staring at the band and slowly nodding his head

Like I am a door into hell

leaning over her on the bed. She was thinking that no matter how sorry he said he was, he would still remember it and not regret it. Not deep inside

In the afternoon we sat on a bench on a plaza near a park.

The last time they drank together he started to laugh at Paddy, for no visible reason. Paddy just smiled at him. 'What?' he said, shrugging his shoulders. 'What?'

✢

And him to see me enjoying it, and I would enjoy it, because it's one of those nasty facts of being human, that fucking is always better when you're doing it to hurt someone, when you shouldn't be doing it, when it's revenge. Even if they don't know about it, even if you're never going to tell them. Even fucking that's feeling guilty and wrong. It's always the best sex. It would kill Axel. I mean literally kill him

✣

I was crying after he told me.

'Brussels, one way,' I heard her say in English through the glass. Seconds later, I said the same thing.

✣

Lucy was engaged to Paddy Kennelly, and she and Trevor were going at it every opportunity they got. They had fucked out here in the Phoeno in Paddy's car, which Lucy often borrowed. That time they were playing Paddy's New Order CD, *Power, Corruption & Lies*. Trevor had drunk with Paddy a couple of times since he'd started riding Lucy.

She laughed again, as if making light of it. I laughed too. I realised I had drunk too much coffee and was succumbing to the nameless dread this often afflicts me with.

It was so fucking cool

✣

47

some installation she saw where it was video games, but you fired real guns at the screen

✻

clouds came in, and it got colder up there. Most of the people went away, and the boy fell asleep on a couch under some jackets. She rolled a cigarette and pulled her chair to the edge of the roof.

sometimes choosing their destination only when they were at the railway station

Karen peered into the mass of pigeons. She said, 'I had a dream that you tried to strangle me.'

I don't remember returning to the hostel.

✻

She could see all of Berlin, or the east at least. She thought of all the other rooftop parties that were happening in the city that night, that morning, and also all the sex people were having, in apartments and houses, with the curtains closed or open, all the unfaithfulness and break-up sex, the revenge sex and bad sex and amazing sex, awkward sex and kinky sex, and also people falling in love. Or some girl, she meets two guys at a party and they all go to bed together, but her friend is going home alone. How many orgasms were being had at that very instant, a kind of life energy rising out of the city, or just a useless vapour and meaning nothing, a

Mia Gallagher

Mia Gallagher is based in Dublin. She writes novels and short stories, and has also worked as a theatre performer and deviser, a screenwriter and a script editor. Her debut novel, *HellFire* (Penguin Ireland, 2006), was widely acclaimed and won the Irish Tatler Literature Award (2007). Her short fiction has been published in the UK, US and Ireland, won the START Award (2005) and was shortlisted for Hennessy, Fish and Trevor/ Bowen Awards. Her theatre work has toured widely and she has enjoyed several writing residencies at home and abroad, including Writer-in-Residence with IADT/dlr (2009-10) and a two-month residency in the Centre Culturel Irlandais in Paris (2015). Mia has received several Literature Bursaries from the Arts Council of Ireland and has also been grant-funded for her theatre work.

In responding to Dave's invitation to write about contemporary Ireland, Mia chose to adapt this extract, part of a longer novel exploring ideas around how people create identities for themselves, both collectively and individually, and what happens to these identities at times of crisis. Themes she hopes will resonate with a 'nation' – whatever that is – which, at the time of writing, is supposedly 'recovering' from its latest crisis.

This is an extract from a novel, *Beautiful Pictures of the Lost Homeland*, developed with the kind support of the Arts Council of Ireland and a residency with IADT/ dlr Arts Office.

17:57:39–20:59:03

<record>

Is there a better story I should be sharing with you? A tale from another lifetime, another universe even? A sci-fi epic with a big cast of characters and interwoven plots? A story that jumps from place to place and spans decades, that's packed with gizmos and technology, plot twists, heroes and villains and enough alien life forms and strange planets to keep even you listening? Instead, I offer you this: a hotchpotch of memories, my own talking head, intercut with reality footage from a day in the life. Mar, if he was still around, would be appalled. Am I avoiding something by telling you this? Playing for time? If I get the chance, will I move on, start talking about other things? Or is this as good as it gets?

That elephant, still crashing around. I'm no wiser, I'm afraid, as to what I'm going to do with your gift.

I sat in the cab, a rod of tension morphing into a brittle puddle as, behind us, the hospital and its infernal machinery, its lost souls wandering in circles, peeled away. I felt not exactly human, but animal again, mammalian, warm-blooded, grateful for the heating, the support of the seat, the thin strap across my chest protecting me from sudden accelerations, the music playing on the sound system. Grateful too to the cabbie, for his lack of surprise at the sight of my face, for not saying something like 'You been in the wars?' or 'Jaysus, that's a rough day you had,' and most of all for his body, shielding me from the windscreen and the knives hiding in it.

The flu had come back, but was keeping its distance. I couldn't smell, but could imagine the smells around me: fake leather, pine-tree freshener, stale tobacco, an after-tang of vomit. The cabbie was wearing a baseball cap; his face was saggy, his eyes hooded. He had Neil Young playing: 'Powderfinger', a ballad of young lives lost, sad and thin.

His eyes flickered in the rear-view, met mine.

'You sure about this? I mean, I can drop you at the station.' There was a smartphone near the dash. His fingers were hovering over it. 'There's a train at nine, and ....'

I shook my head. 'It's grand.' My voice sounded croaky.

The cabbie nodded. His fingers had yellow tips. A box of cigarettes nestled beside his phone. Ninety minutes to Dublin, non-stop. No chance of a smoke. No wonder he was so jittery.

'Eh—I know this is a bit, em, cheeky, but could I have one of your cigarettes?'

He blinked. On the back of his seat, facing me, was the No Smoking sign.

'I won't tell.'

He made a snorting sound that might have been a laugh. 'Alright then.'

He pushed the gearstick into fifth as we swung onto the motorway, then, without looking around, handed me the pack.

'D'you want one?' I asked.

He grunted. I slid out two fags. They were John Player Red, pure lung-rot. Yet another thing you don't know about me: I started smoking in college, where my aunts couldn't see me, but gave up six years ago when I started to transition. I was worried about the risks: circulation, clotting, complexion. Typical, Mar said. Worried too, though I didn't admit it, about the other C, the big one, my mother's legacy.

I lit a fag with the cabbie's plastic lighter and handed it to him. Then I lit my own. Fuck it. In for a penny, in for a pound.

The smoke pushed into my lungs, warm and cushiony. My muscles loosened, my eyes half-closed. Out the front windscreen I could see the road, a blurry grey sea split by a wedge of green, dotted with red tail-lights, the pale silver of oncoming daylights. Behind it, the sludgy blue of the sky. Rain washed across the windscreen, followed by the sleazy tango of the wipers. Ah – one – two – three. The rain had slowed since I'd had the crash. The wipers were better than my Fiat's: they were intact.

A medal was dangling from the rear-view; St Christopher on a blue thread. A picture of a smiling baby was stuck to the front passenger glove compartment. On the seat beside me was a paper, the previous day's *Evening Herald*. No mention of the bomb in London or the looming reprisals. No mention of anything.

The cab swung into the fast lane. A sudden change in my field of vision. My heart stopped, waiting for the cabbie's back to lurch towards me, the glass to break over his face.

One fag, two fag. A good distraction. I watched the world pass: sea, sky, the tiny oblongs of ferries and carrier ships glinting on the horizon. The hills of Wicklow, watery green ex-NAMAlands

scarred newly red by the teeth of JCBs. Brown signs pointing to Scenic Routes, Areas of Natural Beauty, Heritage Sites,
TV Towns, service stations begging for our custom, offering
Cappuccino and Hot Snacks in lime-green, custard-yellow, lip-
stick-red neon.

On the sound system Neil Young segued into Willie Nelson,
then Johnny Cash. As the nicotine worked on him, the cabbie
turned chatty. He was originally from Dublin, he told me,
outside Tallaght, you could probably guess from the accent, but
he'd moved the family to Gorey during the boom. I'd read news
stories about those waves of migration; working-class families,
usually with drug problems, being shifted out to the sticks. Bríd
had wanted to do a programme about it. Ethnic cleansing by any
other name would smell so sweet.

We talked a bit about the weather, then he brought up the
bombing. 'Unbelievable,' he said, and tutted. 'D'you know anyone
over there?'

'No,' I said, trying to flick away the uneasy sensation that I
did.

'Oh.' He sounded disappointed. 'Lovely place, London.'

He avoided mentioning the parade, or what either of us was
planning to do over the long weekend. He must have had me for a
loner; at best, a spinster. On the dashboard, his baby's face stared
at me. It looked confused, like babies often do, and its mouth was
stained with jam. Beside it, in the little digital window, I could see
my fare mounting. I thought of my shrinking savings. I thought
of the fee I'd wrangled from Bríd. In for a penny. I lit another fag.
In the front of my mind, I put it down to the accident. People
get reckless when they've had a brush with death, do all sorts of
uncharacteristic things.

Johnny Cash finished, and then we were listening to the news.

'... man found today in the Royal Canal had a distinctive tattoo on his back, and ....'

'I thought they'd forgotten him,' I found myself saying.

The cabbie tutted again. 'Poor tosser. Took off his face, you know? A torture thing. Sick fucks. They reckon it was kids.'

'It probably wasn't,' I said.

The cabbie's eyes flicked. 'They put it out on YouTube. Has to be.'

'Oh,' I said, remembering the spam I'd got that morning. The cigarette suddenly tasted foul.

'It's all them video games, Grand Theft Auto, zombies ... poor bastard. You'd of hardly known about him what with everything else going on. Chose the wrong day for it, eh?'

'Mmm,' I said, and leaned back again into my seat.

As we reached the border between Wicklow and Dublin, the first signs of the bubble began to appear: For Sale and Development Opportunity signs pimpling out from brown fields and half-finished tower blocks. A never-used arts centre proudly proclaiming its new hooker status: Recently Acquired – Retail & Residential Use. Your world: building sites and half-constructed things, hunks of glass and concrete, shimmering above slatted wooden walls. Jesus, Geo, Mar had said when we'd arrived in Ireland, if they could build on the fucking sea, they would.

Was he right? What would have happened, do you think, if the boom hadn't burst? At the Tiger's height, I used to imagine my city, which used to be yours, all the small cities of this small island, continuing to grow, extending out onto the water until they were floating, like Venice or Lake Titicaca. It may happen yet, if this bubble that everyone's so anxious to deny keeps tumouring, the price and fingerprint of capital. Can you see it, that watery half-imagined world? You used to tell me you were good at picturing things that hadn't been built yet. I imagine it again now, my aquatic metropolis. Tower blocks on stilts, or suspended from wires, strung between the highest peaks of opposing land masses. Everyone swimming to school or work, travelling in gondolas or barges or tiny little tugs with outboard engines; abseiling, even, between the high-rises. Voices calling to each other across the water, crystal clear. Semaphores instead of Facebook. Meetings interrupted by ocean swells as all those beautiful office blocks built by the Tiger and its bastard cub sway, tall glass ships rising and falling, following the rhythm of the tides sweeping in across the Irish Sea. Unbolted boardroom tables sliding across the floors, chairs tilting back like swooning lovers, paper, pencils and corporate toys tumbling off desks. I used to imagine the people too, those new amphibians who would populate our spreading archipelago. They'd be sleek as seals, fat and prosperous, gently proud of their terminally expanding fortunes and never-falling house prices. I liked to think of them mutating, growing strange new organs, internal spirit levels, webs between their fingers and toes. Can you see them too? Getting on with their days, laughing at the sea's interruptions, shaking their scaly heads in easy good humour, while at night their gilly children lie in bed, rocked to sleep by the ever-moving foundations of their floating city, dreaming of a past lost to them, when people walked on solid ground and took balance for granted.

Can you see their mothers, pushing back their hair, smoothing their foreheads, singing land-shanties to lull them to sleep?

Can you see her still? In your dreams? Aisling, my own dream-mother?

Eskimo kiss, sweetheart.

The road was bristling with signs. 60. Slow. Road Works. Flashing lights. A blur of luminous yellow jackets, orange diggers, white helmets, ripped-up ground.

'M50,' I said.

'Sorry?'

'We'll be faster if we go along the M50.'

The cabbie looked as if he were about to argue, but something in my face must have stopped him. He shrugged, soft and helpless, and did what I asked.

The traffic was crawling. The lower parts of the M50 had flooded.

'Sorry,' said the cabbie. 'Wouldn't of thought, with the bank holiday and all ....'

'It's all right,' I said. 'I suppose we could have taken the N11 and gone along the canal. That might have been faster.'

He frowned as if I'd said something stupid; as if he wanted to say something. He changed his mind. 'You ever been to Spain?'

'Sorry?'

'You know, Spain. *Viva España?*'

I shook my head, then remembered. 'Once. I was in Barcelona.'

He looked back at the road. 'I'm heading to Andalusia. Pal of mine has a bar there, so I reckon, if he can do it, you know.... No money in this game any more in spite of what they're saying. Not outside Dublin. Where I am now, Gorey, Wexford, the odd job in Wicklow, but apart from that, nothing. And nights. Jesus.

They're a cunt—' He glanced back. 'Sorry. Hard, I mean. The stories I could tell you.'

Would I be one of those stories? Had one of them he-shes in the car the other night; Jesus, should of seen the state of it....

'I used to rake it in during the good times. Me brothers hated me for it.'

He laughed. I looked at the cars beeping and crawling around the Tallaght exit and wondered how long we were going to be stuck there.

'They all fucked off to England in the eighties. Got jobs on the black working dodgy hotels, giving three addresses to the DSS. Nice money for nothing. Wouldn't blame them. Back here it was a cunt of a place.' This time he didn't bother apologising for his language. 'If they'd stayed, they could of ended up getting in with the wrong crowd, the drugs, all that. I was okay though. I was the babby, born at the right time.' He laughed. It had a dry, rattly sound. 'Used to call me Jammy Noel on account I had it so good in the boom and all.'

He finished his fag, stubbed it out.

'Then my luck ran out. Got busted for a hit-and-run in 05, couldn't drive for six years. Drunk. Fucking gobshite. That learns you real fast, but.'

Did I imagine it or did his eyes drift to the picture of his confused, smiling baby?

He gestured to the box of fags. 'Go on, have another.'

I lit up, inhaled.

He had turned silent and was looking at me. I became aware of the street lights picking out my features, my cuts and bruises.

He cleared his throat. 'Sorry. Gerry, that's my girl, she hated me smoking. Told me I'd get cancer and die on her. Hah.'

I closed my eyes and only half-listened as Jammy Noel told me about Gerry, the girl he'd loved, the girl who was the mother of his jam-faced baby, who'd run off with some fucking Polack or Serb or Russian, one of them gangsters involved in them illegal poker dens on the North Strand. After her ma died she'd legged it real sudden, and they after moving to Gorey for a cleaner life because she'd been messed up before, you know, on the drugs, only he'd helped her clean up, but she hadn't listened, and in a way, he said, if she had taken him back, left that Russky cunt and come back to him, he probably wouldn't even be thinking of going to Spain. You can forgive anything, can't you, if you've a bit of love in your life?

Swish-swoosh went the sound of his wipers. My eyelids dropped. By the time we passed the Red Cow exit I was asleep, not even half-aware that something was wrong.

Martin's face loomed. His eyes were huge and hollow, his skin smouldering. Bits of it were peeling away, turning grey and flaking off, as if he were made of newspaper. Stop, I told him. Go away. But he wasn't listening. The flames licked, caught the ends of his hair, shrivelled them to tufts. Behind him was a dark shape, broad, no head, arms stuck out like one of those cartoon railway signals at level crossings. A door opened. A blur. A gap. We were in a bedroom, my old bedroom in Marino. A window was opening, and....

The world jerked. My body shook. Something was touching my right breast.

I opened my eyes. Jammy Noel's face was close to mine. Too close. He was twisted around, half out of his seat, and his hand was on my shoulder. Martin's coat was unbuttoned. The cabbie's mouth smelt bad. Could I smell? I tried to speak but nothing came out.

He blinked. 'Sorry about that. Didn't know you were asleep. We're, eh, here.'

The cab had stopped. I could see the yellow of the hazards flashing in the side mirrors; suburban gardens, pebble-dashed walls.

Jammy Noel's hand was hot, pulsing against my body. What had he——Had he been *at* me?

My skin crawled. My throat gagged.

He flushed and took his hand from me. 'I'd of woken you up sooner, but you looked like you needed the rest, what with the ....' He gestured to his face. 'Anyhow ....' He glanced at my chest. An involuntary movement, a tic.

Perv. I pulled Martin's coat closed.

Outside, a cherry-blossom tree was moving in the wind. Bare branches, like a woman's arms.

'That'll be €120.' At least he had the grace to sound embarrassed.

I dug around in my coat pocket. Martin's coat pocket. I found my purse, took out my debit card. He swiped it. We avoided eye contact. My head was starting to ache. I stared at the No Smoking sign on the seat-back in front of me.

'Grand,' said Jammy Noel.

I nodded, and smiled a tight smile that made my face hurt. If he hadn't been so dodgy, I might have wished him good luck in Andalusia.

Another tip for you. Trans rule number one: never alienate. Not unnecessarily, at least.

I got out of the car. The rain had softened. Behind the windscreen the cabbie's face had become a fright mask, his eyes black holes, his mouth a vortex. I slammed the door. The lights inside the cab winked out, making him disappear.

I turned, and it was only then that I realised where I was. The kerb was wrong, too clean; the road too wide; the house was similar, yes, that 1930s' pebbledash, but....

'Stop!' I turned, shouting. It was too late. Jammy Noel was already rounding the corner, heading back to Wexford.

I watched him go. Then I turned, pulling Martin's collar up against the rain, and faced the dirty-grey sky and, black against it, the house you'd bought in Marino the year before I was born.

Most things from my childhood shrink any time I've revisited them as an adult – Clonmel, my aunts; your mother, my tottering wreck of a granny; my other grandparents and their two small, tidy graves, packed neatly away in South County Down into two different cemeteries. But our house seemed far larger than I'd remembered it. The windows were dark, the gate ajar. I wondered who was living there now. The front garden looked okay, tidier than when we'd had it, but not as nice as the rest of the houses on the road, with their uniform sandy gravel and weeping birches. They'd put wooden blinds on our windows. I felt a bit sorry for the house to see they'd chosen standard ones from Homebase, not the posh sort with the wide slats. For Sale, said a sign sticking out of the hedge.

Why on earth had I brought myself there? I felt unhinged again, like I'd felt earlier that day at the lakes when I'd seen those creepy teenagers. I felt broken, as if part of me was still in Jammy Noel's car, sleeping, while the other stood here, facing—

What?

It had been nearly thirty-five years. The college I'd gone to had been nearby, but I'd never returned to our road, our house.

Funny, said Mar. Classic addict behaviour. Sorry? I'd said. He'd laughed. Keeping your fix close at hand, Geo, but not touching it. But that doesn't make sense, I'd thought. How could the past be a fix?

I stepped back and looked up. The blank eye of the bedroom window you used to share with Aisling looked back at me. Where was she, that ten-year-old child I used to be? Sleeping, quiet, in her own bed, or had she sensed my approach and woken, crept into your room, and was even now staring out at me? What was she seeing? The person she'd always dreamt of becoming, or someone else?

I peered through the other windows, but I couldn't see anything. It was hard to tell if anyone was still living there. Perhaps the owners had already decamped. To Andalusia, maybe. I imagined them leaving in a rush just before I arrived, escaping before the banks got them, leaving food uneaten on the kitchen table, beds unmade, clothes hanging in the wardrobe. What would they have taken with them? Pots and pans, a mattress, some bread? I remembered my mother's clothes hanging in the wardrobe after she'd left us: pressed trousers, cheesecloth blouses, office skirts, maxi dresses swirling with the colours of the seventies, orange and brown. Her white mac, her Afghan coat. Her rings, her bangles, her beads, her precious things.

Valuable.

I thought of the package you'd sent, the one Dolores had tried to give me that morning. Your last birthday card had been one of those jolly ones about how I was getting older, with a tacky cartoon illustration on the front. Whose idea had that been? Helen's? Sounds like her, so cheerily American. Inside, there'd been a terse message. It could have come from anyone, except it was in your handwriting, grown shaky and frail. An old man's hand, practically illegible. Followed by two typed pages of uninteresting bullshit from her. As if I cared. 'Maybe, when you get a chance, honey, you could come visit?'

Yeah, right.

You'd put my initial on the envelope. G. Madden. Just the G., no name, so you wouldn't be condoning whatever damage you thought I was doing to the life you'd given me. You'd sent a postal order for $100. I'd torn the whole lot up: letter, card, money, smarmy invitation.

Mar used to hate it when I did that; he'd start coming on all Glasgow, blood-thicker-than-water shite.

Jesus, Geo, he's only trying to ... he's family, you know? He's your faither.

Well you're not, Mar, so shut up.

Why d'you find it so hard to forgive him, Geo?

Forgive? I'm not bloody blaming him. Christ, I'm not that much of a child. I'm willing to take responsibility for my part in everything.

Doesn't sound like it. Sounds like—

Like what? Like I'm trying to be right again? I'm not, okay? I'm just—

Just what, Geo?

I looked away, towards the house next door that used to belong to Mrs Kelly. The cherry-blossom was enormous now, stretching over the railing. They'd cleared the rest of her garden around the tree and replaced it with gravel, widening the gate so they could get an extra car in. They'd put the expensive blinds on her windows, leaving them half-open so I could see in. It looked nice, empty and tidy, nothing like our lounge used to. The blinds of the window above were closed. A blue light flickered through the chinks. Someone stood, and for a moment I saw their silhouette through the cracks, all bones and angles like a monster from a German noir.

A sudden nagging unease between my shoulder-blades, a wobble in my legs. I steadied myself. In the corner of my eye I could see the bin near the odd little crossing at the top of the road. It wasn't the same bin, of course; it was black and square, twenty years old at the most. The wind was flirting with a piece of newsprint, sticking it to the bin's side, peeling it off again. Something trembled in the depths of Martin's coat, vibrating against my skin.

'Eejit. Fuck off, will ya!'

A hoarse voice from the corner. Barking laughter. A scream, melting into laughter, from the other end of the road. Pincer movement.

Let me remind you, because it's too valuable a lesson to forget. Trans rule number one: when in doubt, when necessary, hide.

I ducked through our gate and squashed close to the hedge, crouching low. Through the branches of Mrs Kelly's cherry-blossom I saw them appear, a gang of boys from the lane, a pack of girls from the green. The boys were lanky and spotty, the girls luscious and dolled up, faces painted, bodies poured into spray-on jeans and fluoro tops. Put it away, hen, Martin used to call out at the muffin-top pyjama girls in Inchicore, taunting them when they slagged him off for being a queer, though by then he was living with a woman.

Kids. None of them could have been older than fourteen. I felt vaguely ashamed for panicking. Still, as Sonia says, you never can—

'Headcase!'

The girls were shrieking. One of the boys had lunged forwards towards the hedge where I was hiding. Had they seen me? He yanked at the cherry-blossom. I shrank back. Through the twigs I saw a long jaw, mouth gaping like a hyena's. The branch broke; the hyena disappeared. Something released at the back of my head, and my nose began to run.

'Jesus, Macker!' A girl moved into sight, sharpening under a street lamp. She had a perfect mouth, and a heart-shaped face. The hyena-boy laughed, dug a plastic Coke bottle out of his tracksuit and trailed it along Mrs Kelly's railings like a xylophone.

'Scarlet!' said another girl, plainer, blonder, fatter than the first. The boy with the xylophone laughed again. Making a big show of ignoring them both, the heart-faced one tossed her hair, and let her eyes brush over the cherry-blossom, the jasmine, me.

Kids, the cabbie had said. They'd tortured that man in the canal and torn his face from him.

Hysteria, I'd thought. Probably a gangland thing, but the media had gone for the old reliable Hooligan Theory. When in doubt, blame the young.

'Fuckin cunt!' One of the boy's mates had grabbed him, and was wrestling the Coke bottle from him.

Heart-face was still staring through the cherry-blossom. Could she see me?

The lads got into a headlock, to cheers, jeers, and giggles from the girls. The first lad shrugged off his mate. 'Fuckin rotten here so it is. I'm off.' He looked at Heart-face.

She turned, still pretending not to see him. 'Ya drinkin that, Stacey?' A fumble in a handbag, a bottle held high. A cheer.

Stacey drank, throwing her head back, flaunting her formidable cleavage for the boys.

You've got so soft, he'd said, cupping my right breast in his palm. There'd been a strangeness in his touch. Something different in the skin-on-skin between us. Is that okay? he'd said. My Mar, usually so sure with his hands. I didn't know what to say, so I'd just fired the question back at him, like I'd learnt from my therapists. Is it? He flattened his palm, sliding it away from my breast towards the hardness of my sternum. I'd felt his blood pulse, his cock soft against my belly.

Geo, I don't know if—

I pushed him away. Fuck off, Mar.

'Come *on* will ya!'

Stacey was now pulling at the first boy, Macker. But he had eyes only for Heart-face, who'd taken the bottle and was drinking from it, her white throat rippling, her perfect décolletage gleaming under the street lamps. The second boy grabbed the Coke bottle and banged it loudly.

'Bren, leave them railings alone!' shouted Stacey. 'Fuckin *pervert* lives there!'

'Huh?' grunted Bren.

'Come *on*,' said Stacey.

Heart-face was right up close to Macker now. Somehow, an agreement got itself made. The group's allegiances shifted and, flocking, they headed off.

She turned around just as I straightened up, and looked back at me.

'It's not your fault that ya look like that,' she shouted, right at me. 'Scarlet for your ma for having ya!' Then, louder, 'Pervert!'

A laugh from that perfect mouth. The gang howled and she disappeared.

My head was spinning, snot streeling down my face. I kept having to wipe it away with my sleeve. Fairview was a blur of opening pub doors, green bunting and people in stupid hats, belligerent smokers holding court beside tall ashtrays that looked like pillars from Egyptian temples, screeching trad music, streaking headlights, drunks and more drunks and more drunk again. There was a phone box near the corner of the Howth Road. I'd used it as a teenager during my college days. It was missing some Perspex near the bottom; the wind was cold as it gusted through the gap and up around my legs.

'Sonia?' My teeth were chattering.

'Hello?'

Relief surged through me. 'Sonia, hi, it's me, I'm ....'

'Hello?' Everything was noisy behind her.

'Sonia, you're breaking up. It's me, Georgia ....'

'Where are you, girl?'

'Sonia, you're ....'

It took us three goes, and ate another hole in my purse, but finally we connected.

'I was in hospital.'

'Oh. Jesus, Georgia, was that today? I thought it wasn't till—'

'No, that's still tomorrow. I didn't ... I left. I had an accident.'

'Georgia, Christ ....' Her voice disappeared.

'Can I stay with you?' I hadn't planned to ask that. 'It's just, it would be great if—'

'Oh, I'm sorry, girl, I'm ....'

She was in Limerick for the holiday, spending the long weekend there. Family time. Christine and the kids. Of course. I'd forgotten.

'Oh.' I was horrified at how small and needy my voice sounded.

'No, no,' she said, regrouping. 'Look, I have—'

She broke up again.

'... idea.'

'Yes?' I said, desperate. Was I desperate?

'Take a cab.' She must have moved, got the phone into a better signal, because suddenly I could hear her. I felt like saying: A cab? But I've just spent—

'Don't worry about the cost. Give them my account number. I've a spare key ....'

Crackle, crackle.

'Under the what?'

'Geranium.'

'No, no,' I said. All around me were monsters in enormous gold-buckled green hats. 'I'm grand. I should go home, it'll be—'

'Get. A. Cab. You can have a bath. Remember the code?'

A bath? I only had a shower at home. I nodded, then remembered she couldn't see me. 'Yeah.'

'Stay there and give me a ring tomorrow morning, first thing, don't worry how early it is, and I'll give you a pep talk before you go in, and just, you know, just keep ringing, okay? I'll try to get back up early. Christine's supposed to be coming up on Monday with the kids, but she'll understand. Help yourself to what's in the fridge.'

'Thanks.'

'If you need a change of clothes ....'

Behind her voice I could hear people laughing and talking. Trad was playing there too. She sounded like she was in a pub.

'... push it a bit, girl,' she was saying. 'There's a problem with the rider. Once you get in, keep it on the latch and don't let anyone in. Okay?'

The new cabbie was Nigerian. Black. I assumed he was Nigerian. Maybe he was from the Ivory Coast. He had a set of rosary beads dangling from his rear-view. I don't know what religion they are in Nigeria. I mean *have*. What religion they have in Nigeria. Religions. Plural. Aren't they mainly born-again? Maybe he was Senegalese. He didn't speak much. We swung down the coast road into town, and the rosary beads swung in front of the windscreen. Protect me from the knives, I prayed. We passed the park where I'd cruised in the eighties while I was at college, when I first explored the possibility that I might have been gay – no, when I first explored the possibility that being gay would explain why I was the way I was. It was dark and dirty, not a soul to be seen beyond the first ridge of trees.

Over the Tolka, down North Strand, the same route we used to take in the Cortina in the seventies, when you used to bring me to your office, before you decided you were too ashamed to bring me there, or I was too much trouble, or something. Drunken people were everywhere in spite of the rain, careering in messy, straggling groups, raising beer and cider cans at our windscreen. It was only 9 p.m., I could see in the cabbie's clock, but the fights were already starting. Amiens Street. A Garda car was parked outside the Luas station near Connolly, hazards on, blue light flashing. Across the road, outside the amusements arcade Mar had more or less lived in during our last months together, two big, shaven-headed lugs, Russian or Polish or – maybe Jammy Noel was right – Serbs were doing the no-you-can't-come-here-without-a-warrant tango with two obscenely young-looking Gardaí.

The Nigerian didn't say anything.

We crossed Butt Bridge. Over the tops of the roofs I could see the big wheel outside Government Buildings. It was lit-up and turning. The air was thick with the sounds of hurdy-gurdy music, samba bands, shouting, drink.

The cabbie leant forward and pressed a button.

'... no, no,' said Blessed Eoin. He was on a news analysis programme; he sounded panicky. 'I'm not saying that at all. All I'm saying is, this is perhaps a last opportunity for us to understand that violent actions take place in a context, and—'

The cabbie tutted and turned off the sound.

Up Westland Row, then a sharp left down Grand Canal Street, past the registry office where Mar and I used to fantasise we would one day tie the knot, that ridiculous bourgeois ritual that Ray and Ben, our one-time friends, were celebrating, maybe at that very moment, over in Brighton. Past the bridge stretched Northumberland Road. Behind it, unseen, roared the coast.

Colin Barrett

Colin Barrett was born in Mayo. His debut collection of short stories, *Young Skins*, was originally published by the Stinging Fly Press in Ireland. It won the 2014 Frank O'Connor International Short Story Prize, the 2014 Rooney Prize for Irish Literature, and the 2014 Guardian First Book Award. His short story, 'The Ways', was longlisted for the 2015 EFG Times Short Story Award. His work has appeared in *The Stinging Fly*, *Five Dials*, *A Public Space*, *The Guardian* and *The New Yorker*.

Doon

Doon Minion straddled the ivy-covered back wall of the outdoor handball alley, his T-shirt wadded around his fist and his legs hitched tight against the concrete. The back wall came thirty feet off the floor of the alley, and the height made Doon's body concentrate. He could see off a great distance. Beyond the squat brown sprawl of the town lay the grey line of the approach road, on which traffic glimmered like midges on water, then the miles of rucked acreage grading into the furrowed densities of the coastal mountains. The sky he was in was cloudless, the noon sun ticking against his pitted shoulders like a second pulse.

Doon was seventeen. He was waiting on his crew. The handball alley was cordoned behind a rotting fence along a rise on the edge of the town's industrial estate. It was the crew's regular meeting spot. Doon was the leader, and he liked to get there early, liked to establish himself, and so become the thing towards which the others were moving.

The industrial estate was warehouses with corrugated roofs, haulage containers beached on blue gravel, eviscerated machinery piled against walls. There was one human visible inside the estate's perimeter, a spindly sham in a shining high-viz vest moving with a burdened lollop along the main road. The sham was wielding a stick with a pointer or pincer attached, forking trash from the storm drains and transferring it into a long sack that hung like an udder from his waist. Doon wondered if the sham would spot him should he look up, but figured he would be difficult to spot: he was unmoving and slim, and the sun's intensity would reduce him to a reedy quiver at this range. Doon thought to text Mason and ask her to take a photo from ground level as they arrived, so he could see how substantial or not he looked up here, sitting in the ivy. The ivy smelled like leather or varnish. It spilled along the back wall in clotted nests. Doon picked at a vine, its leaves dark-sheened and minutely veined.

The crew would come on their lunch break. Doon was on the doss, though he still went to school almost half the time, which he considered dedicated given that he could get away with not going at all these days. Now that it was in the bone, the ma no longer had the stamina to scourge him out of bed in the mornings, but it was still worth heading in now and then to watch the conviction drain from the teachers' faces. Doon had his special adversaries, the faculty so bereft of backbone he considered it a duty to torment them, the choicest among these being O'Domhnaill, the geography teacher, with his *as-Gaeilge* surname, his highlight-tinted hair and stress-induced speech impediment. Doon made it a point of principle to be in class every Tuesday at three, ankles crossed and mounted on the table as O'Domhnaill blinked inanely behind his glasses and tried to quell his stammer for long enough to order Doon to t-t-t-t-t-take his f-f-f-f-f-feet off the desk.

His back was getting too hot, but that was good. Doon's shoulders were gouged with acne. The burned skin would peel tonight, turn purple and untouchably tender, sheets tacking to him like loose dressing, but that was good. He wondered if he would struggle to sleep, the way the ma did all the time now. Since the cunts in the county hospital had told her it was in the bone, all she did was sup tea and watch TV until deep into the night, and no matter how late she went to bed, she still rose remorselessly at 7 a.m. on the dot.

'What is it, basically?' Doon had asked Dylan, the older bro, a few days ago. They were at Dylan's kitchen table, Doon watching Dylan smoke a joint. Dylan sold hash, sold to Doon and Doon's friends, but appeased his conscience by the infliction of minor proscriptions upon his younger brother: Doon could get high, but not in Dylan's presence.

'Basically ...' Dylan plucked at the pleat of his philtrum, sniffed, sat up, '... it's a swarm of cells that start multiplying too fast. Cells going mental, feasting on you. Your immune system gets muddled, starts attacking itself. It thinks your cells are in revolt, so it goes into revolt against them.'

Doon thought about this, and eventually Dylan said, 'What?'

'Sounds like sci-fi,' Doon said.

He heard Mason's voice, and remembered he'd meant to text her. He braced his legs against the wall and watched them come into the alley, Keeney's long, pale hands spidering between the bars of the gate, its hinge creaking as he turned it, Keeney's peanut head, followed by Dearbhla Mason with her hands in the pockets of her bomber jacket, stomping agilely between the filth to keep her boots tidy, Mullen – the looker, Mason's fella – pushing his hair out of his eyes like he'd just woken up.

'Well,' Doon said.

'Come down you cunt,' Mason said, her voice made big by the walls.

Doon scooched backwards, scudded down the slant of the side-wall, dropped into the court.

'What's the *scéal?*' Keeney was lighting a cigarette.

Doon pulled himself into his T-shirt, shoulders prickling at the lukewarm drop of the cotton.

'No *scéal.*'

'We skirting by Dylan's?'

The crew was in love with Dylan. Dylan had told Doon to keep them away as much as he could.

'Not first. First I need to see Cassie.' Doon scrubbed his hand across the springy fuzz of his scalp.

'Got your haircut like two minutes ago,' Mason said, not looking his way. She raised her hands, palms out, and Keeney lobbed her his pack of cigarettes.

'Two weeks back, now,' Doon said.

'Serious, you don't need another cut.' Cigarette perched on lip. Hands out again to receive the lighter.

'I get it cut so it never needs a cut.'

'Loves himself, I'd say.' She lit up, lobbed the items back at Keeney. Keeney caught the cigarettes, botched the lighter.

'You hurrisome bitch,' he moaned, picking it off the ground.

'Not my fault you got *lámhs* like oven gloves, spa.'

Doon smiled. Mason was congenitally mouthy. He liked her for it. The boys tended to follow Doon's mood, going laconic if he was. Mason's propensity to carp – at everyone, but especially at him – reminded him that he was Leader.

'In fairness, that's a shit way to spend lunch break, watching you get a haircut,' she said.

'In fairness,' Doon said, mimicking her lilt, 'skip a class. We'll head to Dylan's after.'

Doon watched a wasp bobble down out of the air and land on Mason's arm. She followed Doon's gaze back to herself, and rotated her wrist to see what he was looking at.

The only human Doon permitted to come near his head was his cousin Cassie Neary, a bartender in Quillinan's pub in town. Cassie's weekday afternoon shifts were deep with downtime, so all Doon had to do was text ahead the mornings he required a fresh skinning. Number two, all over, every fortnight. Cassie kept a home kit – plug-in electric razor, numbered blades, plastic-rimmed pocket mirror and shaving brush – stowed under the counter, just for him.

The haircut took place in a cramped chipboard and brick extension at the rear of the pub; on weekday afternoons, practically a private chamber. The extension housed a single large pool table. With its varnished panelling and cleared felt surface, the table looked to Doon as substantial and solemn as a casket in repose. He took one of the scarred benches pushed against the walls. Mason, Keeney and Mullen stayed in the lounge, feeding coins into a decrepit arcade game.

'You're awful scalded. Were you out in that all day without sunscreen?' Cassie said.

'A while, just.' Doon said.

She was standing above him, watching him fidget with an unlit cigarette he'd bunked from Keeney. 'You want to, go ahead. It won't bother me.'

'Nah,' he said.

'Do.'

'Nah.'

'Do.'

'You're not allowed smoke inside any more.'

Cassie flounced a dish towel, dressed it across his shoulders. The cotton of his T-shirt was gritty against his skin. 'You're like a babby, having to be talked into doing what you want to do anyway,' she said.

Doon dipped his head, sparked up. 'I'm a babby,' he said.

'I only said, like.' Cassie said.

Cassie was all business once she started: no chat, the skinning banged through with indelicate efficiency. Doon liked this. Head canted, he watched Cassie wordlessly enter and leave his field of vision, watched her expression as she worked, her face blank but intent.

Cassie had cut his hair for years, but beyond this regular arrangement, founded on the allegiance of blood-ties, he did not really know his cousin. Cassie was twenty-four, she'd a kid named Molly, she'd bartended here full-time since she left school. She was a good sort, abiding, one of those ones that never said no to any reasonable request. Sometimes, in a surge of kin-solidarity, Doon considered suggesting to Dylan to cut her in on the business. A sweet-natured doll with an unblemished reputation could make a bomb flogging hash in the province's clubs. Cassie herself would probably not go for it, but Doon wanted to say it to Dylan anyway, to prove to his brother he could think about things, discern potentials.

The door into the lounge was open, the arcade game on the other side of the doorway but off to the side, so Doon could hear but not see the crew, the voice of Mason chastising the blurting, beeping machine as the razor groaned like a wasp behind his ear. The warm, tined touch of the blade, the quick, wedged strokes against the bony round of his skull, was lulling. Doon watched the smoke spool up from his knuckles. He felt precarious and drowsy.

'How long I been out?' he muttered.

'Hah?' Cassie said from somewhere above his left temple.

'Did I not flake out?' he said.

'I don't know, hon,' she said. She clicked off the razor, stepped back. Doon, eyes closed, could hear things being put down, picked up off the bench. Cassie dusted his head with a shaving brush. Frizz sloughed over his ears, his eyelashes. Doon took a drag off the cigarette, which had smouldered down now to almost nothing, and felt placed, returned to himself, as the smoke dispersed through his system, the nicotine humming between his temples.

'Let's see your eyes,' Cassie said.

He blinked, wetness in his lashes. 'That's the smoke,' he said.

'You look spaced,' she said.

'That's the smoke,' he said. 'I'm as clear-headed.'

He stepped out of the shorn hair fanning the floor, dimped the cigarette in an ashtray perched on the flyspecked sill behind him, snapped the customary fiver from his wallet.

'How's your mam?' Cassie asked.

Doon gripped the black rubber cup of one of the table's corner pockets, pressing his bony fist into the cavity.

'The usual pain in the hoop,' he said.

'That's good.'

'It is.'

He considered the pool table's felt surface. The first funeral Doon had ever attended was Cassie's father's – his uncle Roddy's. Roddy was a younger brother of his ma, and his relationship with Cassie's mother had ended before Cassie was even born. Roddy had subsequently lived on his own, and died when his council flat went on fire. No open casket for obvious reasons, though at the time – Doon was, what, seven? – he'd refused to connect his uncle with the sealed wooden box ceremoniously lumbered out of the church and dispatched into a hole in the graveyard. Roddy'd been in his mid-thirties, and had existed for Doon as a habitual domestic presence, materialising at the house on afternoons or early evenings, installing himself at the kitchen table in his pulverised leather jacket, stinking of fags and crushing through a trio of tinnies as the ma fixed dinner or washed up. The pair would goad each other into flights of ire inspired by Doon's da, or a neighbour, or some fella down the pub Roddy was temporarily on the outs with. Roddy had the intricate social life of the inveterately jobless, and always much to relay. He had terrible skin, a face streaked with eczematous welts as bright as burns, and Doon now thought of those vivid purple markings as a portent of Roddy's manner of demise. Not that Doon could believe it, after it happened. There was the catastrophic evidence of Roddy's flat, the window burned out and the brickwork scorched. But Doon could not believe that his uncle was in the box. He thought, even now, that Death should not be so abrupt, so chaotically improvised. Death should be an extended and earned process, befitting of its significance, like acquiring a driving licence or finishing school. Then Doon wondered if that was a heretical thought.

He looked at Roddy's daughter. Cassie smiled, snapped the dish-towel from his shoulders and flicked it at his head. The dish towel landed on his crown, the material a sudden cool cowl covering his neck and eyes. Doon laughed, startled by the accuracy of Cassie's action. 'Dyou mean that?' he said, his words muffled by the cloth. Cassie said, 'What?'

Doon closed his eyes, pressed the nubbled damp material into his sockets with sufficient pressure to make the darkness begin to spark, then pulled it away.

Cathy Sweeney

Cathy Sweeney lives in Bray, Co. Wicklow. Her work has been published in *The Stinging Fly* and the *Dublin Review*. She is currently working on her first collection of short stories.

Three Stories on a Theme

[1] The Web

I was drinking schnapps in a bar with a woman who used iodine instead of lipstick to redden her mouth. When she spoke, the skin between her breasts folded and unfolded like paper. I remember nothing else, except the story she told me.

When the woman was fourteen she fell in love with a clerk who worked in her father's shop, but she was forbidden to marry him because he was poor. So she married a man thirty years older than her; a man so dull that no one could doubt her love for the clerk. The woman was not unhappy with the old man. At night she sat on his lap knitting shawls while he pretended not to be aroused. They had a child, and the old man was grateful.

Years later, the clerk returned to the town and sent the woman a note. They met in a hotel. Taking off her clothes, the woman was conscious of how much she had aged and how cold the room was. They made love, and afterwards the woman went home and warmed her feet between the old man's thighs.

I too have a story on the theme of love. Maybe I told the red-lipped woman my story in the bar that night, but I don't think so.

I was already drunk when she sat down beside me. I am unusual in that regard. Drink makes me taciturn; it is sobriety I have to watch out for.

My story concerns my late wife, and took place in the summer of the great heat when weeds grew totalitarian and trees oozed sap in an endless dream. In dark alleyways spiders built webs of steel. It was so humid I shaved my body hair and took off all my clothes, and for a moment the universe was a magnet placed against a fridge. But nothing lasts. Night is banked against day: night, then day, night, then day. I was nineteen years old, married, and madly in love.

A web had grown in our kitchen. At first spindles gathered in the orifice where the wood had cracked, but soon thick radials felt their way over dry brick. By mid summer I was manoeuvring around it to make pots of coffee. The web purported some great change, but what it was I did not know.

Then my wife got stuck in the web. We were, as I have said, madly in love, and I desired to see all sides of her: the cool side, the kitten side, the side driven wild in extremis. So I left her in the web. The only problem was her mouth. It kept moving. Words slammed around the kitchen like knives against plates. On the second day I could bear it no longer, and placed flypaper over her mouth. The paper was sticky on both sides, and her mouth was soon covered in hard little raisins.

At night I walked the streets to consider the import of having a wife stuck in a web. The idea, so bright and ebullient on conception, had developed grey tones, and the stillness of the river on those nights was soothing. In low light only barges disturbed the stillness, the river indivisible in blackness from the blackness of land, the night silent as glass.

My wife became wilder, and on the fifth day I untangled her and fed her chicken soup. She soon regained her physical strength and became more energetic in her affection towards me, bestowing the kind of pleasure one expects to pay for, and also pain, for she developed a habit of hitting me hard on the mouth. Once, when the edge of my tooth tore her lip, she kissed the tart blood warm between us. In the time we had left we had many other trysts, but none as successful as the web.

My beloved wife died some years after that. She was knocked down by a tram not far from the bar where I met the red-lipped woman. In the depth of my despair I tried to encourage spiders to build another web in our kitchen so that I could relive the beauty of that time, but the spiders ate the sugar I left out, and expired without grace.

[2] Mad Love

Not long ago, a friend of mine who had been asked whether or not he liked pornography replied that he did, but only the pornography made up to and including the silent movie era, which ended in the 1930s. My friend is a dreamer; a lover of doomed women who ride carousels in the rain.

I love my friend. His heart is red, and velvet curtains swish through his imagination.

He has never had sex. How could he? There are no heavenly creatures. No damsels in distress, no blushing maidens, no mademoiselles in petticoats. No dark hair to be let down each night and brushed a hundred times with an ivory-handled brush.

My friend says he does not mind not having sex. I believe him. I tell him sex is overrated. (I am married.)

My friend and I meet occasionally in a red bar in the city. We drink too much brandy and talk in sentences that would mean something if they were not so broken.

We order food from the bar menu and eat very little of it, craving only to smoke. My friend is a great smoker, and I cadge cigarettes from him all evening. He understands. (I am married.)

We smoke like they did in the era of silent films, holding our cigarettes like wands and arching our wrists, our mouths pursed into cherries as though no one had ever heard of Freud.

The last time we met, my friend confided that he had bought a peep show machine. They are, apparently, collectors' items, and cost a fortune. We drank another brandy and strolled out onto the terrace to smoke a cigarette. I asked my friend to tell me more.

His fingers trembled lightly – one finger was yellow from tobacco – and the grey, curly ash dropped from his cigarette onto the floor. This is what he said:

Small, transportable peep show machines were very popular in the early decades of the twentieth century. After a coin is inserted and a crank is turned, an internal light bulb is illuminated and a timer started. Numerous erotic photographs are then displayed sequentially, presenting a flickering motion picture while one looks through the viewer. The pictures can continue to be viewed until the timer runs out and the light bulb goes dark.

He also said this:

While you look into the peep show machine your legs grow stronger and your arms spring with muscles and your torso broadens. Air fills your lungs. Your arteries redden, and your organs oxygenate until you feel you are made of iron. Your neck lengthens, your eyes brighten, your breath becomes deep and sweet. Finally, your hair thickens and your joints become supple and lithe, as though coated in oil.

That night I had a dream.

I took a smooth glass jar, full to the brim with coins, and poured each one into a peep show machine until I grew so strong that I took my wife, stretched out in a red dress, into my arms and carried her up in the air and far away. We floated weightlessly, entwined in each other, like exaggerated dancers in an old black-and-white film. But when I looked down the woman in my arms was not my wife, but some actress from a television advertisement for cigarettes.

I don't see my friend very much. (I am married.)

[3] The Girl who was Made of Paper

Here's a story for you.

There was once an old couple who, after years of marriage, had a child. The people in the village were astonished. The old couple did nothing but read books all day, and even worse, write books. Their house was made entirely of books stacked together to make thin, colourful walls. In the pub the men made jokes about old bulls and old cows, and laughed until their teeth cracked.

At the beginning of spring, when the old couple wheeled a pram out, the villagers looked eagerly into it, expecting a monstrosity, but found instead a child made entirely of paper – a pretty child, but most definitely made from paper, a fine-woven manila parchment sculpted in the most delicate origami. Soon all the villagers looked in the pram, and their reactions wrote themselves in words on the child, words like strawberry and blossom and pearl, words that scrolled as music and danced in ink and disappeared again like water.

The villagers accepted the child as one of their own, and the old couple were delighted. They called the child 'Girl', which the villagers thought lacking in imagination, but soon enough, like all names, it suited her.

And life returned to normal. Girl went to school and played on the swing in the park and grazed her knee and got the mumps and learned to sing silly songs and tell white lies, just like any other child. The old couple were indulgent, a little too indulgent some said, but Girl grew and grew, and every year she grew more beautiful. New words formed on her, words like chrysalis and peaches and cobalt, until soon the men in the pub stopped laughing and stared into their drinks until their eyes froze.

It was after this that the trouble started. At dinner one evening the word breast fell from Girl onto the table. Girl's mother said nothing and cleaned up the word with carbolic soap, but a few weeks later another word turned up in the bathtub, touch, and shortly afterwards one was found in the bedroom, blood. Soon, words were falling from Girl wherever she went, words like sweet and ripe and cherry, making her blush, while the men in the pub whistled until their trousers split. And it got worse. Girl tried to ignore the men in the pub and run around the village as easily as she always had – a little too easily some said – but more words began to stick to her, words like loose and tease and fast, words that no matter how much they were washed left a stain of red. The old couple were worried. They heard whispers in corners.

One night in the deep of dark the old couple stole into Girl's bedroom and wrapped her in the thinnest of thin gauzes, so thin that Girl could not see it, but so tight that no words would ever come from her again. And they never did.

I've forgotten how the story ends.

Perhaps Girl sat at home by the fire, year after year, not knowing that she was wrapped in gauze, but feeling a choking sensation around her, until in the end she dampened and moulded and pages dropped from her like leaves from an autumn tree. I don't believe the rumour that in the end the old couple burned her – heaven forbid, people are not savages – but maybe it is true that, year by year, day by day, hour by hour, she sat closer and closer to the fire until one day she just slipped in.

Eimear Ryan

Eimear Ryan was born in 1986 in Co. Tipperary. Her stories have appeared in *New Irish Writing*, *The Stinging Fly*, *The Irish Times*, *The Dublin Review*, and the Faber anthology *Town & Country*. Her awards include a Hennessy First Fiction Award and an Arts Council bursary. She lives in Cork.

Retreat

They resolve to take off their clothes. Only the method is undecided. The writers want to play strip Scrabble; the artists want nudes to paint. The lone actor suggests strip charades, but nobody is listening. Mark feels he should intervene.

'Would it not be easiest to go the classic route? Strip poker?'

There's a burst of laughter around the kitchen table until they realise he's serious.

The feminist poet clears her throat. 'You don't mean ... *you* want to play, Father?'

'Well, if the rest of you are.' The sharpness in Mark's own voice accosts him. 'Why not?'

The feminist poet makes a face, her mouth tarry with wine. Almost every place setting has an open bottle in front of it, maybe three-quarters empty. The retreat attracts drinkers. After hours of confronting their own work, everyone seeks solace in wine.

'Hold on now. This could get complicated.' The accordion player from Connemara sits up straighter. 'Are we talking Texas hold 'em? Or five-card draw?'

'And who strips? The player with the worst hand?' asks the essayist, a WASPy New Englander who keeps insisting on her Irish roots. 'Or everyone bar the winner?'

The idea is out there now; it has a life of its own. The dinner dishes are cleared to create more elbow room. The feminist poet is rooting through the dresser drawers for a pack of cards she swears she saw earlier. Chairs squeak on the tiles, knuckles crack. Mark tops up his glass and wonders if he will be asked to leave.

There's something unsettling about the term 'artists' colony', Mark thinks – something teeming and ripe. There's an energy in this place that puts him on edge. Even the frogs he encountered on his lakeside walk earlier seemed in on it, hopping around his feet, all puffed up for mating season. He tried not to step on them as he picked his way through the dead leaves.

He's been scrawling his strange, fragmented lines in a notebook for about a year now, feeling guilty about it, guarding it the way a teenage girl would her diary. Applying for the retreat felt momentous, like a vocation or a coming out.

At least he's among fellow misfits here. They have all devoted themselves to the perfection of a narrow art form. There's a boy who makes pencil drawings of ears, pages and pages of them, and talks passionately about their swoops and curves and lobes. There's a percussionist who plays the bongos and performs something called 'human beatbox' as her party piece. They all have odd working habits and rituals, like the WASP, who constantly nibbles sunflower seeds while she writes. When she's wrist-deep in an essay, she tells him, she can go through six packs a day.

The WASP is the only one who calls him Mark. The others all say Father, even though he isn't wearing his collar, and most of them are atheists anyway. The actor felt the need to announce this on the first night: 'I'm an atheist, just so you know.' When Mark said fair enough, the actor got grouchy; he'd wanted to rebuff Mark's religious overtures, and was cheated out of his game.

Mark has never quite got used to the way people see him – as other. At worst, he's a degenerate. After all the church reports there were a couple of slurs shouted at him in the street; he wore his collar less and less in public. At best, people regard him as they would a precocious child. He once overheard two women discussing him at a christening: 'God, he's pure normal! He just chats away to you!' He's usually only called Mark if there's more than one priest in the room, and even then it's an addendum: Father Mark, Father Seamus, Father John.

The others are knitting close together in that summer camp way. He's seen it happen over the last couple of nights. After the initial jolly nervousness – the what's-your-names, the what-do-you-dos – they're drunkenly arguing about politics and sharing joints on the patio. But there's a friendly reserve when it comes to Mark, a conversational neutering. Earlier, the accordion player sat down beside him and declared that this weather could do anything and talked about the colour of the sky for several minutes. The previous evening, the shy sculptor confided in him that her room might be haunted because the rug kept changing position. She measured it with a ruler, she told him; it was definitely moving. For a moment he was worried she was going to ask him to perform an exorcism.

In the midst of the politeness, he can feel a steady pulse of malevolence from the feminist poet. It intrigues him. He suspects it has something to do with when she introduced herself as Emily and he remarked that it was a fortuitous name for a poetess. 'A poetess!' she spat. 'Spoken like a true member of the patriarchy.'

She leaned in closer, elbowing into his personal space. She is, he realises, his favourite.

Emily shuffles the cards. The sculptor looks dubious. 'We're not actually going to play strip poker, are we?'

The boy who draws ears fans his cards. 'Well, we could always play for money,' he says, and everyone laughs heartily.

'But it's not really fair on Father Mark,' the sculptor persists.

'I'll be fine,' Mark says. 'Priests have very good poker faces.'

This elicits more nervous laughs, but it's true. If there's one thing this life has taught him, it's emotional restraint. You can't show fear in the house of a teenage suicide, not in front of drawn faces quaking for answers. You can't cry at funerals, or show your anguish at a young bride shackling herself to a shovel-handed brute.

His feelings are nearer the surface these days. The writing is partially responsible. It has unhitched something in him, even if the lines he writes are sometimes so obscure as to seem nonsensical. They're like a child's chant, set down more for the sound of the words strung together than for their meaning.

But they're necessary. They ease the yearning in him. He has so few opportunities simply to touch another person that even the brush of fingers in the passing of a milk jug leaves his skin tingling. He tries not to thrill at the lurid touch of parishioners' tongues as he feeds them communion. He was once driving on the motorway, and the flash of lights from a fellow driver, acknowledgement for allowing them to pass, brought on a sudden elation. Thirty miles later he was pulled into the hard shoulder, weeping without knowing why.

✻

They play the first hand. The accordion player loses and takes off his jeans with Christmas-morning glee. Emily deals again; she has a card-shark's way with the pack, stacking and boxing, bending the cards to her will. This time Mark has a lousy hand. Anxiety stirs through his mellow three-glass buzz. Is he actually going to disrobe in front of these people? Priests are suspected of every depravity nowadays. Besides, the fact of his celibacy is there in the room like a rising damp, making everyone uncomfortable.

He loses. The table squints at him.

'You can take off your scapular, Father,' says the percussionist. She's trying to be kind, he knows. He lifts it from under his shirt, from where it nestles against his chest, where she knew it would be. All priests wear them, just as all soldiers wear dog tags: to mark you out as a certain kind of man.

There was a teacher at Maynooth – Father Kilfeather – who spoke in military terms. Foot soldiers of Christ, he called them. Recruits. They all thought he was mad, but Kilfeather was right in a way. Only they were more like conscripts, some of them, designated by their mothers to be the priest in the family.

Father Kilfeather was dead set against nudity, too. They would need all their wits about them, he warned, to battle the easy permissiveness of modern society. And not so modern – even lightly eroticised depictions of Saint Sebastian enraged him. Of course, there were rumours about Father Kilfeather – that he liked to strip boys to their waists and then go at them with a birch rod. Sometimes it was a whip, or even, in one story Mark heard, a hurley. But the boys involved were always friends of friends or students from a couple of years ago, and Kilfeather's supposed predilections remained a cautionary tale, something to snigger about after dark.

Mark remembers discussing Kilfeather's doctrines with John, back when they were seminarians and tentative friends. They were nineteen and knew nothing, but liked to talk as if they did.

One of them said – he couldn't remember who – 'But surely it isn't wrong to admire the body if it's God's creation? In a purely aesthetic way? The way you'd admire an athlete in peak condition.' Or perhaps: 'If I'm in a museum and I'm looking at a Grecian urn with two lads wrestling on it, am I doing something wrong?'

Now they are six hands in, and the clothing is forming a ragged pile at one end of the table. The sculptor has lost two hands in a row and is daintily shoeless. The boy who draws ears has pulled off his T-shirt, exposing a pale, flat, hairless chest. Emily sits at the head of the table, having also removed her top. Mark can't help staring; her breasts are magnificent. When she laughs, which is often, they shiver fleshily on the lip of her bra.

They play on. The WASP slips out of her sundress. The actor unhitches his belly from his belt. The percussionist is one of those new-age types, swaddled in scarves and layers; when they tease her that she's cheating, she strips down to her underwear, her face glowing with the daring of it all. Mark takes off his sandals and splays his toes on the cold tiles. The wine runs out, and the accordion player produces a bottle of brandy.

Flush, flop, three of a kind – even the lingo is filthy. It's been so long since Mark played poker, and it shows; he hasn't yet won a hand. He's already removed all his outer clothing. If he loses again, he'll have to show skin. When was the last time someone saw him naked?

He blinks at his cards. Two of clubs, four of diamonds, five, seven and eight of spades. He plays out the hand with white noise in his head. He should have folded when he had the chance. He's at the mercy of these people and their smartphones, practically offering himself up to become the next Twitter grotesque. What has he been trying to prove? That he's 'with it'? That he's just like them?

When he loses, Emily whoops. He curses, takes a sip of brandy, and grabs the neck of his shirt.

'Sorry, Father!'

The sculptor has her hand up, palm out, as if to say 'halt'. She isn't looking at him. He freezes, still holding his collar.

'It's just … are you sure you want to be doing this? This is all great craic and everything, but aren't there rules against this kind of thing?'

Emily is smirking. 'Yeah, Father. Thou shalt not expose thy nipples to thy neighbour.'

'Jesus,' says the sculptor. 'Well, if I'm the only one who finds this degrading ….' She stands up too fast and stumbles out of the kitchen, murmuring, 'I do *not* need to see that,' under her breath.

'You forgot your shoes,' the WASP calls after her.

Mark is still standing, unsteady on his feet. Emily looks straight at him, her dark eyes drawing him in. 'Well, what are you waiting for? Off, off, off!'

The boy who draws ears takes up the chant, and then the actor, and then they're all at it. Mark disappears into the black of his shirt, then emerges.

There was a time, with John. It was turning from muggy summer to crisp autumn, and the change in the air was electrifying.

They were on retreat on the Beara Peninsula, older now, close to ordination. They were staying in a cheap hotel room with twin beds. They walked back from an evening meditation, energised and smiling and full of back-slapping optimism.

'Remember Kilfeather?' John would have said. 'Remember his little hobby? The cudgel?' Mark's rejoinder: 'I heard 'twas a cat-o'-nine-tails!' They had been like that all night, nostalgic and foolish. Then John turned to look at him, with a perfect poker face: 'I can show you the scars later if you want.' They laughed again, but nervously this time.

When they turned in, John said he might like to shower. It struck Mark as odd, the way he announced it. Mark undressed and got into bed. He could hear the swish of the spray in the next room. He turned away from the door to the en suite and pretended to be asleep.

When John came out of the shower, all was quiet. He did not pad around the room; it was as though he were standing there, looking down at Mark. The air was charged, and words were passing between them, all unspoken, all on faith. It would have been so easy to stop pretending to be asleep, roll over, and touch John on the wrist or the hip. And Mark might have known what it was to be known, to be seen.

But he didn't turn over.

The next morning, neither of them said anything, but there was a distancing after. He hadn't thought of John in a long time. What parish was he in now? Mark had been told, but he'd forgotten, maybe on purpose. It had been so long he could probably walk past John in the street and not know.

*

98

The table is heaving with flesh. Breasts, paunches, hips, buttocks. Sexual organs hidden demurely under the table and between crossed legs. So strange to see all these naked people sitting politely as if for high tea. Strange and beautiful.

Mark is down to his boxers now. He glances at his fan of cards. He has worse than nothing this time.

Emily meets his eye. 'All in, Mark?'

'All in.'

He plays. He loses. They cheer when he stands up to slide his boxers down his hips.

'Off! Off! Off!'

He is standing before them, arms outstretched, whole and unafraid.

Claire-Louise Bennett

Claire-Louise Bennett was born in Wiltshire, in the southwest of England. After studying literature and drama at the University of Roehampton in London, she moved to Galway. Her short fiction and essays have been published in *The Stinging Fly*, *The Penny Dreadful*, *The Moth*, *Colony*, *The Irish Times*, *The White Review* and *gorse*. In 2013 she won the inaugural White Review Short Story Prize and received an Arts Council bursary. In 2014 she was awarded a grant from Galway City Council. She published her debut short story collection, *Pond*, in April with the Stinging Fly Press.

Oyster

There was a bear and some other things. I made my way towards its hair, towards the edges of its hair. Some spiders had got there already. That was weird. That was unexpected. They didn't seem to know where they were, they didn't seem to behave differently from any other time I'd seen before. That annoyed me. That made me think of streets and that annoyed me. I blew on the spiders and they ran. The spiders went running across the stones and these lumps, I don't know what they were.

I hadn't been here long I'd only just arrived. My clothes were woven and knitted and riveted and buckled and all about them were many hooks and straps and places to put things. I hadn't been cold yet but I anticipated it. Standing, anticipating the cold, I would look at the horizon as if I might see icy fingers appear over the top, as if the horizon were a railing the icy fingers could take hold of, as if I might witness the cold hauling itself up onto this railing in the distance. As if the horizon were in fact some kind of gate, that anyone could stand upon and take a long look from. But this is a fantasy – the cold is not like this, and neither is the heat. There was heat, now, coming from the bear, but I didn't want it, it was too much, feeling the heat was too much. I remained close for a while anyway. I remained close to the bear for the simple reason that I wasn't ready yet to continue on. There were things up ahead that first I needed to make out.

I knew there was a deer, at least one. I knew there was a goat, maybe three, I knew there were dozens and dozens of frogs, I knew there were innumerable rabbits and hares. I knew there were pheasants and very likely a badger, so many badgers in fact. Big round badgers. I thought of the weight of them all and how heavy they must feel on top of the earth. Lying there with all these motionless organs inside them, motionless. And I'd been thinking about all these organs and I'd been thinking about them for quite some time, for long enough to experience some strange ideas. I found myself wanting to do something with them, to what end I didn't know. It occurred to me that if I collected a few organs and held them, just held them, it would come clear to me. This wasn't something to think through. How could you think through something like this? It was completely outside anything I'd ever conceived of.

I've killed things. I've gutted things. I've skinned things and I've plucked things. I've taken the head and hooves off things, snapped a hundred throbbing necks, dissected the quaint gizzards, removed the twilit scales and gristle, 'til there was nothing left but neat flesh. And then I was ill for a time and had things brought to me and fed to me. Thin insipid pools tilting beneath a marshy scum that lingered on the edges of the hot flavourless spoon. Gaunt vegetable roots and groping strands of meat would occasionally rise up like junk. I received porridge, accepted potatoes, grasped mugs and mugs of sweet blistering milk skin. I quashed lumps of nocturnal bread and occasionally sucked on a small lukewarm knuckle. Sometimes, rarely, there might be something with raisins in it. Raisins and cinnamon, and any number of confectionary diversions that I'd close my eyes and name. It was summer outside and for about an hour each morning the sun was at my window and lit up the room so I could see all the things I was unable to wear or use. Despite this, despite this highlighted helplessness and the languorous frustration that attended it, I liked this hour of sun.

Nobody knew what was wrong with me. Some doctors came, different doctors at different times, but hardly distinguishable to me. They formulated opinions and pricked around with vials and needles and bits of cloth. But they didn't know, nobody knew. I knew. I knew very well and I knew it would be quite some time yet before I'd recuperate. I knew there was no way of expediating recovery. However, it seemed necessary to assure people that solutions were possible so I made up conventional symptoms where really I had few. I said I had a temperature. I said my mouth was dry and my throat tight. I said I'd lost all sense of taste. I said my hands felt clammy and my feet stone cold. I said my eyes stung and my ears tingled. I said today I feel a bit better. I said that many times. I didn't want visitors but visitors came. Below I heard taps running and a broom sweeping and burning coal shift to powder in the grate. I heard singing. Of course the visits became less frequent. Several days would pass without interruption and, during the last stretch, the last long stretch of uninterrupted days, I partook of dreams and visions that were compelling and distressing and invigorating. I sensed a world had been made. In all this time, despite what might have looked like withdrawal and inactivity, I was an attuned host to many magical things – some of which I'd encountered before – and a world, some kind of place to inhabit, was being remade.

Claire-Louise Bennett

There is nothing easy about this. There is nothing easy about this kind of upheaval, of not knowing what goes where. Processes of realisation and change are, most times, tentative and incremental. Like a two-way thing. Like a collaboration. However, sometimes, something from the outside gets in, slams right in, secretes, and creates havoc. For me it was an oyster. There was a plate of them, the customary dozen I suppose, unhinged and relaxed upon a pale blue dish. Exposed, briefly, to the lights, to the sounds, before being decanted into the dark and muted interior of my body. Later that evening I became very ill. Ill in the usual way. There was nothing abnormal or perplexing about my condition, I had food poisoning, it was straightforward. My body contorted wildly in an almost rhythmic sequence of emphatic evictions and ecstatic ejections, like something possessed in fact. Because, I assure you, the pollutants that leaked out inside me were not simply chemical or bacterial toxins. As fantastical as it sounds, I believe the oysters, wide-open upon that small round table, were still in the business of absorbing their surroundings and had become quite enraptured by the lights, the sounds, and the conversation that accumulated everywhere around them. A conversation that passed slowly, very slowly, giving them every opportunity to take everything in.

It was dense, mostly, dense but wandering, containing many things that had not been directly witnessed but had been uneasily imagined. We were discussing evil. A sense of love between a pair of humans makes it possible, makes it tantalising in fact, to link hands and say the devil's name. Not that we were involved in an attempt to summon up any sort of pernicious force, it was simply that intimacy and low candlelight were daring us to share our most contravening thoughts. At the same time, despite the

104

theoretic and expansive nature of the conversation, the exchange was neither intellectually driven nor intellectually received. It was, regardless of verbal poise and execution, quite the opposite. This was, perhaps, a man and a woman exhibiting an atavistic mode of unification. This was a man and a woman whose path towards biological and emotional consolidation had bought them to that damp moss-held bower where breath hangs visible in the air and fear must be admitted and all the shapes and symbols it has taken on in the world are identified and faced. It was a place of vulnerability and appeal. It was a place of terror and assurance. It was a moment when all that is ugly, repulsive, horrific and unfathomable rotated and bobbed like a charred carousel in the slanted air between us. This is what we're up against. This is what's out there. This is what we might ourselves contain. Across the table our splayed fingers entwined. I would have walked anywhere. I would have made a home anywhere. I would have stood with nothing anywhere. And all the while I was loosening the aphrodisiacal filters from their corrugated single door.

The following day we made the journey southwards and I threw up over many places of outstanding beauty. After a while I didn't bother to walk into the trees, I just hung my baneful head out of the car window and stared down as my remnants mingled shamelessly with small stones and grass. The expulsions lasted for days and I felt my body was intent on reversing itself. At the same time, the things we'd spoken of, and the feeling of primal unity I'd derived from the intercourse, endured and created a new and terrifying lining. I was a beast and I felt danger and I felt sickness and I felt that love had suddenly become base and without margin. None of this was communicable, which was a pity and is regrettable because this alchemic and unnerving infiltration wasn't mutually felt. Perhaps I'd unfastened more than my share of oysters. Quite possibly. Indeed, once home I felt and heard hinges twitch and blanched rippling doors close up around me. Cloistered. For a while it was beyond me to know if I were male or female. Within ten days my body recovered more or less but other areas of me did not. Or, more precisely, they didn't return to how they had once been. I began to feel ineffable and freakish and remote. There is nothing easy about this. There is nothing easy about the distance this created. Alone, then. Quite alone, yes. One morning I returned from the bathroom with a towel wrapped about my body. I returned to the bed and remained there, with the towel wrapped tight around my wet body. And it didn't dry, my wet body, not for a long time. So I remained there, on the bed, and the most straightforward explanation for this was to say I felt ill.

There are no clouds. There is no breeze. My attire is somewhat elaborate but I dressed without thinking. I am fulfilling something but I am not hypnotised. There was a bear and some other things. Inert and heavy on top of the earth. Badgers, like big round islands. Frogs like winter's stones. Deer slung into death's warm sack. Rabbits and hares with ice-cold ankles. There are not so many trees, there are few things in fact that alleviate the terrain. And the terrain was heaped with cases containing organs. I crouched beside an animal and opened it up. I could not see very well since there was not much light, within or without, so I felt my way around. And then my hand cupped around something with involuntary tenderness and the thing yielded almost immediately. I looked up and held. The spiders had reached the trees and stood around looking back. I don't know what they were thinking. I continued. My hand moving slowly, deliberately. As if knowing what to search for.

There was nothing random or haphazard about any of this. I was fulfilling something but I was not hypnotised. Indeed, I found that I was applying my consciousness fully to things, the many things that had been undergone. I thought, for example, about making love. I thought about what happens, about what really happens, when a man and a woman copulate, over and over and over and over and over and over again. And it was difficult, to begin with. To begin with it was a very difficult thing to think about – not because it was in any way painful or troubling, it wasn't – but for the reason that I didn't really know what the most effective way of thinking about it was. When I attempted to recall my own direct experience of making love nothing came to me – I could see faces, but nothing else. I would try to isolate a face and close its eyes – I thought if I closed the eyes it might make it easier, easier for the rest of the body to come about. Then, since this had no consequence whatsoever, I thought perhaps I ought to close my own eyes, so that's what I did – I laid down my knife, laid it down by the side of a badger – and I closed my eyes. There was then one face in particular that I could see very well – and it was in fact a pleasure to see this one particular face, and I was relieved and glad that it was this particular face and not another that had segregated itself and was now quite still and clear to me. And, it's true, closing my eyes did bring the face closer, closer to my face, but it was a bit dissatisfying all the same, because although my eyes were closed they were also wide open. Looking at this face, and I just wasn't at all convinced that any of this was the best way to go about thinking about what happens, about what really happens, when a man and a woman make love. So I let go of that and thought of no one – I stayed by the badger and kept my eyes closed, and thought of no one.

I saw nothing, just the blood and the vessels that are there, in that thin slip of skin over the eyes. Such a small and unremarkable piece of a person and yet, seen from beneath, the lids are so vast, so unending, and not for the first time I thought it was strange really that anything anywhere decided to support my spirit such as it is with this architecture of bones and so forth. And then I could feel my bones, I could really feel them – within the fibrous depths of my muscles, my flesh, my tissue, my blood, I could feel these silent gleaming bones. Gleaming. Gleaming. Gleaming within the tumult of my body. Gleaming, most likely, with that luminous dust which dropped down from some assembly of stars a very long time ago. All that way, all that time, in order to kit my spirit out with shape and power and mobility. Little formless weightless spirit. Hoisted into place by a precise arrangement of columns and bowls and spires and hinges and levers and domes and pinions and racks. And then my lips began to move. They began to move for the reason that they were saying something – but without producing any sounds – with a sound that only happened in my head, nowhere else, just somewhere inside me, perhaps my head, I don't know. And the words that I was saying, and which only I could hear, were, over and over and over again. And I said this, in more or less the same way, over and over and over again. I wasn't counting the number of times I repeated it so I don't know how many times it had been said when I began to feel aroused. And then, when I was aroused and unrolling, I carried on, over and over and over again, but it was different, the way I said it now had altered, it was more immersed I think, as if I were moving the sound right over the inside of my throat and jaw, right the way back to my blushed ears. It was such a lavish feeling, over and over and over again, that I just kept on, until I realised that I was, in fact, arched across the badger's back. He was still so very warm. The back of my neck had become hot and my hair adhered like mist. What is it, I thought, to go inside someone. What is it, I thought, to have someone go inside you. Over and over and over again. What happens, what really happens. And what happens when they don't any longer?

By dawn I'd gathered many, many organs. With every pocket and pouch crammed I walked on for an hour or longer and then I came to a river. It seemed to me the first moving thing I'd seen in a long time and I was amazed by it actually, by the whole thing about it – its colour, its motion, its lights, its sound – and especially by it being water. First of all I washed my hands, which in the daylight appeared garish and even a little theatrical. After, once the nails had reappeared, all sharp and infantile, I rinsed the organs off one by one and placed them side by side right along the river bank. It was quite a collection – quite a display in fact. They shone. That was unexpected. They really shone. I had no idea what the meaning of it was, but I knew that was the end – that was the last thing; there was nothing more to be done now. There was nothing more to be done. I turned to the river and took off my clothes. So many straps and ties and hooks and fasteners to undo – it felt inevitable and momentous, not to wear anything. I stepped down into the river and for a while I just floated there and felt the warmth of the upcoming sun. I floated on my back, and felt the warmth of the upcoming sun on my face, on my toes, on my breasts, on my knees, those parts of me that came and went from the surface of the water in a manner so luxurious and free. And then I flipped onto my front, pushed myself deep into the water, and began to swim towards the next embrace.

Alan McMonagle

Alan McMonagle lives in Galway. He has published two collections of stories: *Liar Liar* (Wordsonthestreet, 2009) and *Psychotic Episodes* (Arlen House, 2013). A radio play, *Oscar Night*, was produced and broadcast as part of RTÉ's 2014 Drama on One season. He has contributed stories to various publications in Ireland and North America including *Southword, Grain, Prairie Fire, The Valparaiso Fiction Review, The Stinging Fly* and *The Book Show*. He is an aflame, two-thumbs-up contributor to an anthology celebrating the 'thematic and stylistic splintering' seeping into Irish writing.

The Remarks

We had been living in the flat for almost a year. Three of us. Madigan, Eric and me. Friends by mistake, and poor to boot. Madigan was from the country and always in trouble. Eric was from a small town outside Philadelphia and liked to be by himself. I preferred to keep where I was from a secret, and passed the time trying to quell my urge to steal. Together, one morning, the three of us discovered we liked poteen-flavoured bread.

It was Madigan's idea to soak the bread. Fed up with Eric's miserly attitude, he had dunked one of Eric's loaves into a pan of poteen. And when Eric emerged from his room and took a bite of the poteen-soaked bread, he clasped his hands together and said, 'Hey! This isn't bad.' Then he began to weep. Madigan and I didn't know what was happening to him. He took a bite of bread, and tears sprang from his eyes.

'I've lost it,' he cried, over and over again. 'Don't touch my cap,' he snivelled when I tried to console him by presenting to him the baseball cap he had just whipped off his distressed head. Then, having nothing better to do, I tried a slice of bread and, at once, began to weep as well. I didn't know why I wept, but the tears welled up inside me and gushed down my face. Madigan stared at the pair of us. Then he took some bread, dipped it in the poteen, and as soon as he tasted it, he, too, began to weep.

'Does anybody have any idea what is happening?' Eric asked, wiping away his tears.

'Oh, man,' I said, unable to stem the flow.

'That's it,' Madigan blubbered, and pounded his chest like a gorilla. 'I've had enough. I can't take any more.'

We looked at him. A ropey vein was threatening to rip through his neck. His nose was purpling and starting to throb. His waterlogged eyes reddened.

'I hope I don't look like that,' Eric said, looking from Madigan to me.

'Oh, man,' I whimpered, fighting a losing battle.

'Know what this means?!' Madigan roared, and the vein in his neck almost burst through skin. 'We are space wasters.'

'Speak for yourself,' Eric said, and disappeared into his room.

'Let's go across to Heroes and grab a roll,' I suggested.

'Stuff Heroes!' Madigan bellowed. 'I've had enough of Heroes. I have Heroes coming out my underpants. WE ARE SPACE WASTERS.'

This outburst further encouraged me to get Madigan out of the flat. I managed to tempt him across the road, not to Heroes for a roll, but to Babette's – the second of the two cafés on our street – where I ordered a pair of breakfasts with tea for Madigan and coffee for me. In Babette's, the fry-up set us back €2.95. It came with a basket of thick-cut brown bread and kept us going until teatime.

Over breakfast, once the effects of the poteen had started to wear off, Madigan told me about his dream.

'Someone wants to chop my head off,' he began.

'Who?' I asked.

'A woman. A sexy woman. She's wearing a bikini and has dark skin. And get this. I'm willing. I'm only too happy to go along with it.'

'Really?'

'Yep. I'm not cuffed or shackled or anything. I'm kneeling down, offering no resistance. And she's standing over me in her bikini, ready to swipe with her sword. I have an awful feeling it might be that singer, Beyoncé.'

'There are worse ways to go,' I said.

'What do you suppose it means?' he asked.

'Whatever it is, it can't be good. Not with all the screaming coming out of you.'

'I don't like the dream. I don't like it at all.'

'What are you up to today?' I asked him, thinking it might be a good idea to steer the conversation elsewhere.

'I'm not sure. There's this girl I like.'

'Oh, yes?'

'I might go and look for her. You going stealing?'

'Don't know. Yes. No. Maybe.'

'Get me something if you do.'

'Like what?'

'Surprise me,' he said, and then disappeared.

Madigan disappeared quite often. Eric and I called these blissful spells The Quiet Time. At night, for example, when he went looking for love: 'I'll buy it if I have to,' he'd growl, heading for the door with a determined grimace. 'I might go to the hospital,' he'd say, venturing out into the night, 'I hear nurses are clingy.' Going out, he'd forget his key, and later break windows to get back in, smashing through neighbouring doors. He'd borrow a bicycle to get somewhere and could never remember where he'd left it. He received regular head injuries. Many of these arrived courtesy of the high gate separating Babette's from the bar across the road from us. Scaling it provided access to a shortcut Madigan liked to avail of when returning from his favourite nightclub. In the past two weeks alone he had fallen three times, and each time landed on his face. Into the bargain, he claimed girls no longer talked to him, refused to buy him drinks, showed no desire to join in when he sang his Johnny Cash songs. 'Should it not be you doing the buying?' Eric put it to Madigan quite reasonably one evening. But Madigan had already lit upon another approach. 'I like jazz,' he'd decided he was going say. Later, though, the girls would still run away.

I went back to the flat and played card games for one that I had invented. Part of my strategy to curb my larcenous ways. When I ran out of games I picked up Eric's volume of western philosophy and tried reading a paragraph. When that became too difficult I switched on the TV, and for a few minutes watched a rerun of the most recent *X Factor*. When that became too distressing I just sat there and looked to the future.

I could see the future so clearly. I saw the three of us in a rock band. The Remarkables we were called. Starting out, we set ourselves a number of modest targets. We did free gigs. Support acts. Cover versions sprinkled with tentative offerings we were slaving over night and day. Then Eric had the great idea of dropping the word 'able' and we became The Remarks. That contraction made all the difference. At once, a top record company signed us. We released our self-titled debut album to commercial and critical acclaim. *Rolling Stone* called it an epoch-defying mindbender of an album. 'The Remarks have unleashed a Pandora's box of guilt, despair, paranoia and self-loathing', declared the kind journalist at *NME*. Madigan's drumming was singled out for its controlled anarchy, while Eric's anguished lyrics, underscored by my one-note guitar, caught the mood of a generation grappling for its place in an empty world. The consensus: we were at once depressingly brilliant and brilliantly depressing.

After a while I tried to disturb Eric. Then I stood by the high window taking in the view of our street. Then I sat down and watched the conclusion of *X Factor*, and then the news channel, where Sharon was telling us over and over again about the latest beheading in the Middle East. Eventually it was teatime, and Mary P. swung by with two litres of milk.

Mary P. worked in the corner shop on our street and smoked. Our daily two litres of milk came from the shop. Every day, on her way home, she'd call by. She spoke beautifully and always chose the right words. Her expressions lifted our day, and very often we were uppermost in her thoughts.

'Boys, there is nothing in your fridge,' she said on this visit, having given our kitchen her customary inspection. 'You are neglecting yourselves.'

As she spoke, her cigarette arm protruded like an elegant spout. Over her head, a ribbon of smoke formed a halo. Delicately, she placed the milk inside our empty fridge and promised ingredients to a robust meal.

Along with milk, Mary P. supplied poteen. The poteen came from her uncle's still. We couldn't believe our luck. She brought two litres of milk, a pint of poteen, promises of good food, and placed it all in our empty fridge. I knocked back most of the milk before it went sour, but it was hard to keep up with the regular deliveries. Eric watched me as I drank and shook his head. He didn't trust milk.

'Ah, the very stuff,' Madigan said as soon as he reappeared, and had checked the fridge, nodded approvingly, and got busy with the poteen.

'What are you doing that for?' Eric asked him, as Madigan soaked some more of his precious bread.

'I want to see if it happens again. Here, taste this.'

I did as I was told, and soon the tears were flowing. Madigan laughed, then cried. Eric took a slice of his bread and at once buckled. Throughout all of this, Mary P. stood there, cigarette to hand, watching us blubber.

'What do you make of this?' Madigan asked her, amidst his tears.

'Oh, man,' I cried.

'It still tastes good,' Eric whimpered, like a baby.

'You should tell your uncle,' Madigan bawled, allowing himself to rest against the shoulder Mary P. offered him. 'Let him know he can't be pushing this sort of stuff on people.' Then he stood tall and pounded his chest.

'Tears are the ultimate form of communication,' Mary P. told us, having witnessed our collective reaction to her uncle's poteen. Then she blew us each a kiss off the palm of her hand and left.

Eric was taking a year out before returning to start film school somewhere in California. He had ambitions for this year – his year of self-discovery he was calling it – and, every chance we had, Madigan and I did our best to thwart him. Unlike us, Eric also had money, which was fed at regular intervals via Western Union into the post office around the corner. It was a regular if meagre allowance, and he rose early most mornings to walk as far as Supervalu, where he bought a loaf of white bread for his breakfast. Madigan ate whatever was in front of him, whenever he found it, so Eric was inclined to stash his Supervalu loaves. Things had long since reached the point where, when Madigan and I appeared in the kitchen, Eric would position himself between us and his bread and announce, 'I want two euros before either one of you touches a single slice of that bread.' At which point Madigan turned to me and smirked, his impish eyes already lost in the hatchings of a devil-scheme.

With Madigan out of the way, Eric made the most of the quiet time. In his room, he tapped into his laptop and slurped cartons of orange juice through a straw, emerging once in a while to put on a pot of two-minute noodles, which, along with white bread, formed the main part of his diet. He had a photograph of Hemingway taped to the wall over his bed, and a quotation that went, 'Would you please please please please please please please stop talking?' When he moved into the flat he was halfway through the first page of a screenplay. Months later, Madigan and I were quite certain he was still on the same page. 'Plots don't matter,' was all he'd say when we asked about his story. He seldom gave much away, was protective of everything. His story; the Penn State baseball cap he constantly wore; bread. 'One of these nights I'm going to kick him hard,' Madigan promised me time and time again.

Our second album followed up on the promise of our debut. Titled *Too Much*, within seven days of its release it was an iTunes number one, and this despite our great rival's latest album being made available as a free download. With his confidence on the rise, Eric's lyrics became more combative, while at the same time, Madigan was revealing himself more and more as the loose cannon we always felt he was. On our world tour, in turn, he threatened to set himself on fire, leap from our hotel rooftop and inject himself with a vial of speed. And this last bit during a live performance. Our manager wanted him gone. We took a vote, and he stayed. Eric and I felt that his fatalistic energy offered the ideal counterpoint to our natural melancholy. The fans agreed. Eric even talked about allowing him contribute lyrics to album number three. 'Crippling self-doubt meets absolute narcissism: This is Art', proclaimed *Rolling Stone*.

Overwhelmed by the avalanche of success I was conjuring, I opened the high window and listened for the river. I could hear it, making its way towards the sea. It was dark save for the street lamps. From time to time, a wayward drunk wobbled down the street. A boozy couple warred. Someone kicked an empty beer can or bellowed a name that had injured them. Taxis passed. Time dripped. In his room I could hear Eric swearing to himself. 'Motherfucker. You scum-sucking asswipe of a person. Retard!' I switched on the television. The news channel reported another beheading, this one uploaded onto the internet. I searched uselessly for something else, turned the thing off, drank a glass of milk and went to bed.

When we were hungry again, Madigan and I moved four doors up from Babette's to Heroes. An overstuffed roll set us back a further €2.95.

'We're going to do it this year, lads,' Big Val, the rickety owner, said, setting down our plates. 'It's going to happen. I've a good feeling.'

'Well, it's about time,' I replied. 'We're getting old waiting for us to do it.'

'Aren't we all?' Big Val said, his broad smile lighting up his ever-happy face.

I shrugged my shoulders. Madigan flashed a toothy grin. Neither of us ever knew what Big Val was talking about.

Besides, Madigan had other things on his mind.

'I've had another dream,' he told me, leaning in close. 'I die twice,' he said.

'Sounds rough,' I said.

'I think I get it from my mother. She was always dreaming about death. Funny thing, though, I never remember coming back to life – you know, so I can die again.'

'But you do come back to life?'

'Yes.'

'On second thoughts, that's not so rough.'

'I don't like the dream. It spooks me.'

'Tell it to Eric,' I said. 'He might immortalise you.'

'That lad needs to get out.'

'Did you find the girl you were looking for?'

'Huh? Oh, her. She's a cloakroom attendant in Rumours. Her bloke stands beside her all night. "Watch your face," he said to me. I'm going to have to figure out a way to distract him.'

Madigan had more to say. He always did. About his mother. About his vulnerable face. About his past. He told me about when he was little, how his mother liked handing him to relatives. 'Here he is,' she'd say to his Aunt Olive at the beginning of Easter. 'Don't let him watch any crucifixion films.'

'Well, that explains your dream,' I said when he was finished.

'What do you mean?'

'You think you're the son of God.'

'Fuck off!'

'Yes, you do. You have a Christ complex. Coming back from the dead. Sacrificing your face for the love of womankind. You think you're the son of God, and you want Mary P. to be your mother.'

'Fuck off!'

'You'll be showing me holes in your hands and feet next.'

I wouldn't mind, but he actually checked his hands, front and back. He would have been better served looking out for his noggin. Next time he cleared that gate he was so fond of he was headbutted by an Alsatian and lost half a front tooth. The gap played havoc with his grin. Madigan. Immerse him in a bath of liquid gold and the first thing he would have done was release the stopper.

'I think it's the bread,' Madigan declared during our next visit to the vale of tears.

'Come again?'

'This Supervalu bread Eric likes. That's what's making us cry.'

'The bread?'

'The Supervalu bread.'

'Madigan, what exactly are you saying?'

'We need to try different bread.'

'What? Like Dunne's Stores' Better-Value-Beats-Them-All bread?'

'Yep. We could certainly try that.'

'Tesco bread?'

'Yep. Tesco bread might work.'

'I hear Lidl bread is quite good.'

'And don't forget Aldi.'

'Aldi!'

'Don't knock it till you've tried it.'

'Why don't we just raid a bakery?' Eric suggested.

'Jesus!' Madigan bellowed. 'That's right. Cut out the middle man. Why didn't I think of that?'

And so that night the three of us took a walk as far as the bakery on the western edges of town. Madigan even went so far as to bring a crowbar, which he concealed inside the donkey jacket he was wearing. In the event, his weapon came in handy. The bakery was well manned, the night shift in full swing, and no way were we getting so much as a slice of fresh bread until Madigan produced the crowbar and started steadily tapping it off the bars of the bakery gate. After that, one of the bakers emerged, loaf in hand, and tiptoed uncertainly towards us. When he felt he had come far enough he tossed the loaf over the gate, and we gratefully accepted.

Back at the flat, when we poured the poteen and dipped our new bread, the tears fell as usual.

'I think I prefer Supervalu bread,' blubbered Eric, and went to his room.

'Oh, man,' I cried.

'Well, I think it tastes great,' Madigan bawled, and later that night another sword-bearing executioner must have turned up in Madigan's dream, so loudly and hellishly was he screaming for us to rescue him. When I ventured into Madigan's room, there was Eric, kneeling down beside Madigan, who was on the floor, curled into a shuddering lump of fear and torment.

Madigan was so spooked, as were Eric and me, and so, for a time, we stuck to cheap beer, and to the wine Eric shelled out for. To my amazement, the pair of them even managed to come away from the storeroom of a nearby pub with a full keg of cider. They rolled it to our door and somehow hauled it up the stairs and into our living room, where the three of us sat around staring at it. 'I don't want to know a thing about it,' Mary P. told us when she supplied the taps and gas necessary to complete our very own bar. When we were rigged up, Madigan pulled the first pint and presented it to Eric. Eric sipped, then guzzled, then held out his empty glass for a refill. We opened our door and let everyone know about our windfall. A little later the flat was wedged with an assortment of hippies, buskers, gutter types and ranting poets. And for a time – about four and a half hours to be precise – the three of us were the toast of the street.

For our third album we hired two producers and introduced harmonised guitars, a quartet of backing singers and a string arrangement that included contributions from a renowned cellist Madigan fell for in a big way. Upon its release, to coincide with Madigan's birthday (he was twenty-three), *Feed Your Head* signalled an ambitious distancing from the narrow horizons of our early work. The reviews were generally favourable, if a tad muted, with that formerly kind reviewer from *NME* daring to suggest that we were already forgetting the place of chaotic melancholy that had spawned us. We received requests to collaborate with two Grammy award winners, and were asked to provide the soundtrack to a big-budget movie. A leading gadget manufacturer wanted to run its ad campaign using one of our tunes. We took a fast vote on it and told them to up their offer. They did, and we were soon moving our money to a tax-sensible destination and building mansions in the sun.

For several weeks we hardly strayed beyond our street. I was still trying to eliminate thievery from my life. Eric was immersed in his masterwork. After his encounter with the Alsatian, Madigan's face needed time to heal. We didn't speak to anyone we didn't have to, barely noted the passage of time; if you put a gun to our heads we would have had to guess the day of the week. We didn't even turn on the TV in case we had to endure the aftermath of another beheading.

Summer was in full swing, and with it came more and more visitors, guidebook-bearing couples in raincoats, busloads of North Americans, and always drifters, anxious to while away time in the place recommended to them by drifter acquaintances.

New buildings appeared daily. Red, yellow and green clusters. Made-to-order constructions thrown up at a moment's notice by hatched-out developers. Parts of the city centre started to resemble larger-than-life Legolands. It was a depressing sight, and kept us indoors all the more.

Odd rumours reached us. The Bishop was back in town. Quay Street had been evacuated. The river was high, and fish were in the trees.

Even Big Val got in on the act. 'Want to know what I heard?' he said, tapping his nose. 'The Taliban are in Rahoon.'

'You think that's bad?' Madigan was quick to throw back at him. 'A bunch of Mayo men are after moving in next door to us.'

Mary P. swung by with her deliveries. Milk. Poteen. Recipes for meals that would never get cooked.

'Boys, are you still crying rivers?' she wanted to know.

'Yes, we are,' we said.

'Good,' she said, nodding approvingly. 'There is hope for ye yet.'

Back on the poteen, we took turns preparing the bread. Madigan, in particular, seemed to relish the task. Candles. A clean bowl. Saucers to catch the crumbs. And always a fresh batch of Supervalu bread. 'It's time,' he hollered as soon as he was ready, and we gathered around the candlelit table and beheld the pint bottle of firewater Madigan gripped with both hands and then raised up over his head before pouring into the bowl.

'Here we go,' Madigan said, his tears starting to land.

'And to think I always thought it was an old man's drink,' Eric said, quickly falling apart.

'Doesn't matter. It tastes great,' said Madigan.

'Oh, man,' I cried.

'I've heard it causes blindness,' Eric said.

'And if the wind changes, your face will stay that way.'

'It's giving you nightmares, Madigan.'

'No. What's going on in the world is giving me nightmares. This tastes great.'

'Did you ever find that girl you were looking for, Madigan?'

'I'm biding my time.'

'Mary P. She's the only girl worth having,' said Eric, reaching for a towel.

'Don't be daft,' Madigan said. 'She's too ....'

'Thin?'

'No. She's too ....'

'Pure?'

'No. She's too ... like my mother.'

'So what's the problem?'

'I wonder what it is we are communicating,' I wondered, taking a turn with Eric's towel.

'I don't want to know,' Madigan blubbered and pounded his chest.

'I'm going back to my room,' Eric said.

'You know what his problem is,' Madigan said, sticking his blood-specked face towards me and jabbing my flimsy breastbone. 'He's lost the plot.'

And I took my turn to dip bread, and Madigan took a turn, and at some point Eric emerged to put on a pot of noodles and sat and dipped bread with us, and with the early light breaking through the three of us sat there, weeping our silent way into the pain of another day.

Album number four signalled the beginning of the end. As though aware of the change in our collective mood, not to mention the grandiose pretensions evident in the previous album, we made a conscious effort to return to the glory days for this last, tragic offering. *Beginning To Hurt Again* featured some of our edgiest songs. Instrumentally, we were as effective as ever, if a little unadventurous. But something was missing. We couldn't seem to locate that treasure chest of cohesiveness and purity that had heralded our arrival not quite three years ago. Things came to a head when Madigan and Eric clashed on stage. 'I told you so,' our manager said to me, wagging his ever-pointing finger. And all I could do was smash my guitar over his head and say I was through. We were all through. We had burned brightly, but oh so swiftly. The fans were distraught. Petitions arrived daily. *Please re-form.* But by now we weren't even speaking to each other. Then, one inconsolable fan turned up outside Madigan's sea-view villa, mouthed the words 'I love you', and set herself on fire. After that, there was no going back.

Breakfasts were cheap on our street. We dipped our bread and watched teardrops explode upon guilt-ridden countertops. In our fridge stood forty litres of milk, a half-pint of potato wine and a recipe for everlasting Bolognese. In his room, Eric's ghost tapped out his story, while some shadow's hands dared Madigan's dream to its terrifying conclusion. I filled glasses of milk, dealt cards to myself and waited for the screams.

Finally Madigan succumbed, and hauled himself as far as Rumours. The coat attendant was there. Along with her bloke. And his gang of friends. It was a chance Madigan was ready to take. And so, within earshot of the girl's bloke and his gang, he made an impassioned case for the special time he had to offer. Later, they followed him and pushed his face through the window of the arcade across the road from Rumours. The following morning he was still picking out specks of glass and grinning through his ordeal. 'You haven't seen the girl,' he said when we tried to talk some sense into him. He then dedicated to her the cuts on his face. 'What has she got?' we asked him, but he just sat there, grinning through his open wounds.

And, as I knew would happen, I ventured out stealing. Packaged sausages. Wine. Shirts and shoes. I was better at it than ever. And so I ratcheted up the ante. A cheap bottle of table red quickly became a limited edition Amarone. A

Dunne's Stores' Better-Value-Beats-Them-All T-shirt was overlooked for a John Rocha jacket. Half a dozen pork sausages were pummelled into oblivion and reincarnated as a hunk of prime rib. There were gifts for my flatmates. An inkjet printer and cartridge for Eric. A bicycle for Madigan. Unable to help myself, I was slipping into the inside pocket of Madigan's donkey jacket an eclectic selection of perfumes for Mary P. when I felt the strong arm on my shoulder. The security guard, it turned out, knew my old man. 'A new fool replacing an old fool,' he said to me, shaking his head. Didn't even have the heart to throw the book at me.

A day or two later Eric printed off a ream of blank pages, presented them to us and declared his year of self-discovery at an end. Then he booked a flight home. 'They're cutting me up!' Madigan screamed through his next dream. 'They're cutting me up and scattering me.' And the very next day he announced that he, too, was packing his bag. It was either that or else he was going to throw himself out the high window.

To prolong the agony we decided to cry together one last time. Only this time we couldn't. We poured our poteen into the same bowl we always used and dipped slices of Eric's Supervalu bread and gnashed it down. But on this occasion, our last night together, it seemed to have no effect.

'Typical,' Madigan said, throwing his arms into the air, his face littered with tiny cuts, 'the one time we ought to be crying, we can't.'

'If Mary P. were here she would say we are no longer communicating,' I said.

'I wonder where we'll be this time next year?' Eric said.

To break the ensuing silence, and also feeling I had some experience in these matters, I volunteered a response to Eric's comment, and so I assured Madigan that his days as a space waster were numbered. 'Respect and adulation are coming your way, Madigan,' I said, and outlined the successful career as a percussionist he had ahead of him, and offered a sunny story of his relocation to Australia and the beachfront property he had there and his party yacht that regularly cruised Sydney Harbour. I even mentioned the good times that awaited him with a certain cellist. Of course they laughed and dipped their bread and asked for more, and so I dipped and listed out the gongs Eric's early scripts would steadily accumulate, before he set about reinventing himself as a serious dramatist and finally managed to complete his masterwork. It was well received, won a couple of important prizes and enjoyed a sell-out run in a trendy theatre off Broadway. His leading lady thought him a sensitive genius. He thought she had wonderful hands. 'More!' they bellowed, and I threw in some of my own successes, and how after a botched career as a housebreaker I got my act together and started a chain of Michelin-starred restaurants specialising in molecular gastronomy, and how many successful years later I invited my famous friends around to break bread with me, and there we were, gathered around the chef's table, good food and fine wine, and swapping tales from our perfect lives, not stopping it seemed until we had exhausted every eventuality and all was well with the world again, and then, at last, the tears came, gushing out of us as though there were no tomorrow.

Sydney Weinberg

Sydney Weinberg is an American writer and environmental activist living in Dublin. Her writing was featured in the 2013 Edinburgh International Book Festival's Story Shop programme for emerging writers, and has since appeared in *Colony*, *Minor Literature(s)*, and *Long Story, Short*. 'Omen in the Bone' reflects her fascination with the moral trajectory of identities that span both victim and aggressor, the consequences of emotional illiteracy, and the shabby state of our planet.

Omen in the Bone

I

Her only purgative act was to burn the underwear she'd had on, burn it symbolically on the damp, narrow balcony of her rented flat in south London in the presence of her best friend, Margit.

'I don't care if you're not going to the police,' Margit said, 'but I'm never talking to him again, I swear to God.'

Anna prodded the underwear with a chopstick.

'Look,' she said finally, 'we were pissed. He's liked me for years. I'm not going to ruin his life.'

Margit took a deep drag.

'I know, I'm not saying anything.'

Anna snorted, rubbed her nose. The morning was overcast, blind and vast above them like a polar eye.

'Give me your fag, the flame's gone out.'

'It's too wet out here.' Margit pursed her lips at the death of her cigarette against the crumpled lace. 'Plus your pyre is about to collapse.'

Anna didn't answer. Her eyebrows knit together forbiddingly, a look Margit knew well.

'Let's just go inside,' murmured Margit, her eyes fixed on the smouldering heap. 'This isn't going to work.'

'It is,' said Anna. 'It is going to work.'

A month after the burning of the underwear, Anna took a train to Amsterdam. She'd already exchanged a couple of emails with a childhood friend of Margit's, now a nurse, and so knew vaguely what to expect. I plan to find a job straight away, Anna had written. I recently finished my degree and I want to travel. The Netherlands has always interested me.

The room is €160 a week, the nurse wrote back. I am hardly there, I stay at my boyfriend's a lot. It's an *anti-kraak*, not fancy. Okay?

Okay, Anna thought, scrolling through her phone. Anything would be okay, just get me the fuck out of London.

It didn't take Anna long to find a job in a coffee shop off Dam Square, selling pre-rolled joints and weed brownies to tourists from all over Europe. It was November, and Amsterdam was just as cold and wet as London, only more picturesque and infinitely safer to cycle across. An *anti-kraak*, she quickly discovered, was a soon-to-be-demolished flat the government rented on the cheap in order to keep out squatters. The first time Anna found herself in the house alone, she glanced through all the rooms. It wasn't a comfortable place to live, but she could see how once it might've been. The taps in the bathroom were beautiful antiques, but the flimsy shower curtain was covered in mould, the tiles eternally slimy. The toilet was in its own separate cubicle altogether, lit by a black light that lay prone on the floor. It was true that the nurse hardly ever stayed there. Anna bought a stolen bike for ten euros on Warmoesstraat and flew through the icy rain, freezing and fiercely proud of her solitariness, which seemed to her a necessary stage in her personal growth. She was friendly enough with a few people at work, but went out with them only once or twice, both times going home early.

There was a third housemate. Anna saw him rarely, since he worked most nights on one of the seedier pub crawls. The first time they met he'd shaken hands with her in the hall and said his name was Michael and he came from Galway. He was young, tall and gawky, and gave the impression of a fishing pole balanced precariously against a door. The pimples flourishing along his jaw, however, failed to detract from the pleasant shape of his face or the flecks of eagerness in his eyes. He didn't seem to like Amsterdam particularly, and Anna, perceiving this, felt a kind of tenderness towards him.

It never occurred to Michael that the English girl renting the room next to his had any sort of opinion about him. She was a good five years older, at least, and if he thought of her at all it was because something she once said had bothered him. She'd only been in the flat about a week, they'd run into each other just a handful of times, but still she'd asked Michael what he wanted to do with his life. They were drinking tea standing up in the kitchen and she was only making conversation, so he'd shrugged and said he didn't know. Then she'd given him this scrutinising look and said, 'Well, you don't get anywhere without an education.' That had been the end of the conversation, more or less; she'd walked out a minute later.

It wasn't true, he thought. His dad had owned pubs for years but never gone to college, and his sister had gone to college but was on jobseeker benefits and now expecting a baby. Still, Anna was older, she had this confidence to her, and he'd got the impression that maybe she possessed some important set of information he lacked. He felt that way about most of the people he'd met since abandoning Ireland a week after finishing his Leaving Cert. Moving to Amsterdam was practically a whim – he was sick to death of home, and his mates said it was good craic. The only problem was that he'd come without those mates, and now he was lonely, endlessly hungover, and mostly subsisting off kebabs.

On one of Michael's nights off he came home at around eight, a little stoned, and discovered Anna in the kitchen, cooking. It was icy outside, and the kitchen was cozy and seemed to glow yellow from the lit oven. He'd have to get his mam to send over his winter coat, he thought, sliding past Anna and filling the kettle.

'What's that?'

Vigorously stirring the contents of a pot, Anna didn't look up but said, 'This is polenta, and that's going to be roast veg. I don't know if you'd be familiar with polenta, but it's an Italian cornmeal.'

This answer gave Michael the same unpleasant feeling as when she'd made the comment about education. She was odd but nice enough, he figured. He said slowly that he did know what polenta was – his mam loved Italian food and made a dish like Anna's sometimes.

'You must be hungry,' Anna said.

'You're all right.'

'You don't have to be polite, there's loads.'

They ate in his bedroom because there was no dining table, and his room was where the sofa was. After, Anna rolled a joint and they smoked together. Digging his fingernails into a ribbed cushion, Michael felt the muscles in his face melt into a more relaxed expression.

'Thanks for that,' he said. 'You're a deadly chef.'

Anna smiled and denied it. She had dark, warm eyes that seemed to eat up his words, and so, as they sat smoking and staring into space, he found himself telling her, slowly, why he felt so unhappy. She nodded and listened, and at one point got up and put on nice, mellow folk music he didn't recognise, but liked. Despite the room's bare walls, gaping closet and sagging air mattress, it felt cosier than ever before. He told Anna about the maths programme his mother thought he should apply for, his unwillingness to return to Galway, and his general uncertainty about the future. Whenever he paused, Anna's voice leapt into the ensuing silence and rolled into his ears with a smooth, weighted momentum. Her words were precise and brilliant, he felt, but he was too stoned to retain them; he was left only with the impression of her masterful voice juxtaposed against his wavering one, like a music teacher demonstrating scales. By the end of the night, he understood, she would tell him exactly what he should do with his life, and then he would do it, and be content.

Nodding hazily, Anna said, 'When I was your age I felt really lost too. You just need to give yourself time – to travel and think and read and all that. Do you tend to read? You'll make more sense to yourself if you read, I think. I can give you a top ten list.'

She threw back her head and squeezed drops into her eyes from out of a tiny bottle. All night she'd done this periodically, explaining that her contacts got too dry when she smoked. Michael accepted this more or less indifferently. Anna was a strange creature. Her nose was just a bit too large, her hair black and curly with a pronounced widow's peak. The entire shape of her seemed ill-defined, plumpish, accentuated by big, watery breasts that drew his eye. He could imagine what his mates would say about her and pushed the thoughts away. She was half ugly, half sexy; he couldn't quite figure it out. But she was listening to him, and it felt like a long time since anyone had bothered with that.

He said, 'I reckon if I go back to where I'm from, I'll end up thirty having done nothing for years and years.'

Anna brushed a loose strand of hair behind her ear and dropped her hand where it grazed against his thigh. Michael went on.

'I know I'm really good at maths; it's always come easy for me. But I don't love it, you know?'

'Can I ask you a question?'

'Go on.'

'Are you a virgin, Michael?'

Michael froze. It was his practice never to admit this fact to anyone, but Anna had ambushed him in a moment of torrential honesty. He'd had a girlfriend all through school, but she'd been clear about her limits.

'Look,' Anna said. 'I think you just need to relax. Let's forget about everything and do something stupid, okay? Doesn't grass make you horny? Watch me.'

He watched her as she peeled off her jumper and the top beneath it, revealing breasts minimally contained within a flesh-toned bra.

'Oh,' said Michael, 'that's really nice of you, but ....'

Anna slipped off the couch onto her knees, losing her balance a little and giggling. As she unzipped his trousers she kept her eyes on him. Michael met her gaze and then looked out the window, where, just visible through the darkness, he could make out a cluster of pigeons on the roof opposite.

'Yes,' he said bravely, 'well you're probably right, I might as well do the programme, it's a living. And it's hard to get jobs in this economy even with an education.'

Anna didn't bother responding. He thought maybe it would be best if he hurried up and came, but the strange thing was he couldn't feel anything. So he tried to say something like, 'it's all right,' or 'maybe you shouldn't,' but the embarrassment of it was too much. And she kept watching him. When she finally stopped he thought that her mouth had got tired, and at least now it was over. But instead she climbed on his lap and fitted him into her like an expert mechanic.

'Maybe I should wear a condom?'

'Do you have one?' Anna's voice was breathless.

'No ....'

'Relax,' she said. 'I'm clean and you can pull out; you just have to tell me.'

She pulled his hair back and smothered his mouth with her mouth. Her armpits emitted an odour like rank tea. He winced from the pain of his pulled hair as Anna on top of him moaned and made the little sounds he'd provoked before, experimentally, in other girls, and which had always given him a sense of pride and power. Finally she stopped moving and kissed his neck, and he had the sudden fierce desire to shove her across the length of the room.

'You didn't come, did you?' she said. 'Don't worry; I didn't come my first time either. It's more common in men than people think.'

Then she asked if he wanted another joint, and he said he didn't, and soon after she got up and went to her own room.

In the days that followed, Michael and Anna both worked a lot of night shifts and slept during the day. Michael was not exactly displeased to have dispensed with his virginity. While the memory of the incident itself was not one he preferred to dwell on, he was relieved finally to have joined the ranks of men. It did seem to him like he worried less now. Also, when he talked to pretty girls on the pub crawl he felt cooler, and he laughed at lewd jokes more knowingly. This lasted about a week. Then his mother called to say that his sister was delivering her baby prematurely and would Michael come home, if just for a wee while? But Michael packed all his things, left a note and a week's rent for the Dutch nurse, and didn't say goodbye to Anna.

Months passed, escorting out winter. The baby got bigger; Michael started working as a barman at his dad's old pub in Knocknacarra; flowers appeared in the city centre's public beds. Sometimes, not very often, Michael let his mind drift back to Amsterdam and his aborted life there. Remembering late summer days cycling through Vondelpark, getting stoned and watching swans, it seemed absurd to him that he'd ever wanted to leave. When he found Anna's email scrawled on the back of an old tram ticket, he spontaneously wrote to say that he enjoyed meeting her and hoped she was well. Anna wrote back an hour later, saying likewise etc., and immediately forgot about him. Two weeks later, Michael wrote again:

Sender: ladsitsmichael@yahoo.com
Recipient: anna_c_surrey@gmail.com
Date: 23/04/11

Hiya Anna,
I hope you don't mind hearing from me again, I was just thinking about my short time in Amsterdam and

wondering what your up to now. I got into the maths programme at college, and I start in August. I think it's the right thing for me. Also my sister had her baby, also named Michael, which is a tradition in our family. My dad is Michael too. Anyway, maybe you don't remember this but one time in Amsterdam you were on about books and said you'd write down a list of the top ten I had to read. I'm not too busy right now and could probably look into those books. If you have the time would you send me the list?

Thanks,

Michael

Anna read this email on her phone while waiting to be interviewed for a journalism fellowship with an environmental news website based in London. A blonde woman in glasses opened a door and called Anna's name. She rose, and Michael's email slipped her mind completely.

Michael didn't write again for six months, though he thought of Anna every now and then. It had started to worry him that he hadn't slept with any other girls; he felt himself eyeballing girls like they were deer. Meanwhile, his single encounter with Anna remained strangely magnified in his memory. It had still been light out when he'd come back to the *anti-kraak* and shared her dinner. He'd eaten a plateful, and that was enough. Despite his height he'd never experienced that insatiable hunger which trademarked boys his age. He'd told her that. He had a quiet voice – teachers had often scolded him for it – and on that night Anna had leaned closer to hear him better. She'd always looked at him intently, then and even before, when they'd just exchanged hellos in the hallway or grumbled over how tired they both were. Normally Michael would let his sentences trail off, but the way Anna watched him without saying anything, without filling in the gaps herself, he'd been obliged to go stumbling after conclusions – blushing and embarrassed, but also kind of grateful. He remembered thinking that she wasn't like anyone he knew, in a good way, and had the urge to tell her that. Instead, he ended up writing to her after his mother died.

Sender: ladsitsmichael@yahoo.com
Recipient: anna_c_surrey@gmail.com
Date: 13/10/11

Dear Anna,
I'm sorry to bother you again but the fact is since I last wrote you my mam passed. It was breast cancer but she didn't find out until too late so it didn't take a long time. Before we found out I told her once about you putting honey in the roast veg you made that time and at first she said that was strange, but then she tried it, and after that she always did it. You don't have to write back. I think maybe you don't check this account any more, and if that's true then I can say anything at all, and that's mad. Maybe in the future I'll want to. Michael

Sender: anna_c_surrey@gmail.com
Recipient: ladsitsmichael@yahoo.com
Date: 13/10/11

Michael! I'm so sorry I never got back to you. That's terrible news about your mother, again I'm really sorry for you and your family, she sounds like a wonderful woman. Thanks for getting in touch anyway, it's always nice to hear from you. Write anytime and tell me whatever you like. Things are good for me at the moment – I'm back in London and writing about climate change for an environmental news organisation, here's my most recent piece if you're interested. Sorry again for your loss.

Take care,

Anna

Waiting for the link to load, Michael pictured Anna alone in a small but modern studio flat (this was improbable, he knew, and truthfully Anna shared a four-bedroom house with six others in Greenwich). Nevertheless, Michael's Anna was very confident and successful, with a glossy blackness at the heart of her, a sedentary opalescence, as if she were a fat black spider or a cat, its eyes opening and closing in dissatisfied sleepiness. He saw her sitting immoveable on a cornflower-printed couch – the same couch as the one in his room in the Amsterdam *anti-kraak* – waiting like a cat or a spider or a robot that may or may not be sentient, spewing out devastating articles about the diseased planet.

Michael's phone buzzed. It was his dad. He saved the link, and over time returned to it, reading all of Anna's articles. Every week there were more. There was a small thumbnail headshot that accompanied her name that he tried not to look at. Once he dreamed that he was at his college library, reading her articles, when he felt a tap on his shoulder and it was her. The distortions that had occurred in his conscious memory melted aside and he saw Anna clearly, exactly as she had been. This sudden, unexpected verisimilitude was uncanny and his fear precipitous. He was paralysed in his chair, staring at her. He could feel his heart roving through his chest, tapping dumbly in forgotten corners.

Anna's articles depressed and thrilled him. She wrote about top-secret trade agreements between powerful nations and even more powerful corporations, agreements which gave those corporations the legal right to sue governments over loss of profit. She wrote about the mass extinction of animal populations at unprecedented rates, and the rate of carbon in the atmosphere at which human life is no longer viable. Visiting his mother's grave with his sister, Michael started explaining some of the things he'd been reading.

'Michael, love,' she said, shifting baby Mikey onto her shoulder, 'people have been making predictions that don't come true for as long as there's been people.'

Michael went home to the house he shared with his dad. His dad worked and drank, so Michael mostly had the house to himself. Over time, he started learning how to cook, using podcasts and YouTube videos. When he made root vegetables with honey, it reminded him of his mam and not Anna. He considering taking a leave of absence from college and going off somewhere, Germany maybe, where he could work on an organic farm. But he had the uncomfortable feeling that wherever he might go, Anna would already be there, anticipating him.

II

The last weekend of November, Michael went up to Dublin for a party and met a petite brunette named Jain, who perched on the edge of a couch with a pink drink in hand and told him she was an art student who made dioramas. Her voice was quiet like his, and even when he sat down too, her face assumed an upturned position and she rarely blinked. Draining his beer, Michael cautiously confessed that he didn't really understand art. Jain just shrugged and said that museums were a good place to start. He couldn't be sure how exactly he wound up with her number, but a couple of days later he called.

It was a clear and breathtakingly cold night when they kissed for the first time on Aston Quay, Michael's bus idling behind them. The whole of Dublin dripped with Christmas lights, and Jain, her face swaddled in a voluminous scarf, smiled secretly all the way home.

'It's so easy to be with you,' Michael had told her. Jain ran the memory of him saying this over and over again in her mind for the stab of pleasure it gave her. She thought he had the kindest eyes of anyone she'd ever met, and when he said that he didn't understand art, he was really saying he didn't understand himself. She found this both sad and beautiful. When Jain looked into Michael's eyes, she saw all the sad and beautiful things he didn't let himself understand, and she nearly lost her balance, so great was the rush of love.

Jain shared a large Victorian house in Rathmines with three other art students, none of whom were home the afternoon she invited Michael over to view her dioramas.

'Sorry for the mess,' she said, leading Michael through a sitting room that struck him as fairly tidy. 'Through here ... this is my room.'

He would've known it was her room, he thought, had he wandered in himself, unguided. An IKEA loft-bed stood starkly modern above a faded, antique love seat, while under a window swaddled in billowing mint-green gauze, an old peeling door rested on two trestles and formed a desk. The paisley-papered walls were artfully choked with framed prints that seemed to be illustrations from a Victorian children's book about woodland animals, and a cardigan he'd seen Jain wear once lay on an enormous colourful rag carpet in the centre of the floor. Jain swooped down and retrieved the cardigan, folding it with wonderful deftness and popping it into the wardrobe.

'I'll make us gin and tonics,' she said nervously, and slipped back into the hall.

Michael stepped over to the window and looked out onto the back garden, dingy at this time of year and not far removed from any given back garden in Dublin. Turning back to the room, he thought what a good artist Jain must be, so completely had she translated the ephemerality of her personality into things he could see and touch. No one else could ever have this room; it was too completely hers. And this thought filled Michael with anxiety — that a girl with such a robust sense of self had expectations for him. He felt panicked, as if he'd be required to make a speech once she discovered her mistake.

The door wobbled open as Jain shouldered her way in, her eyes fixed on the two overfull glasses she held extended in each hand. Setting them down on the trestle desk, she grinned triumphantly and then gestured to an object the size and shape of a shoebox, obscured by a black cloth.

'That's my latest one,' she said. 'Will I show you?'

Michael nodded. With a self-conscious half-smile, Jain lifted the cloth and Michael saw in a flash that the diorama was a miniature replica of the room in which they stood. He noted the framed pictures, the loft-bed, the antique sofa, the wardrobe, the desk, even a glass on the windowsill. Except that in the diorama, everything was rotten and broken – the loft bed had collapsed onto the desk, crushing it, and the wallpaper hung in loose mildewed strips from the walls. The floor was strewn with dust-encrusted piles of books and sodden paper, the duvet was black-mapped with mould, and the window was shattered, shards of glass scattered into a meaningless constellation across the floor.

Jain stood on the tips of her toes and rested her chin on Michael's shoulder.

'You know how you said the planet is dying?' she said. 'I got obsessed with that; I wanted to go into the death; I wanted to feel it like it's already happened. I was reading Emily Dickinson, have you ever read her?'

Michael, who didn't remember talking to Jain about the dying planet, closed his eyes.

'Michael?'

He opened his eyes again, and Jain handed him one of the brimming glasses. He felt that she was waiting for him to say something.

'It's really good.'

She suppressed a smile, and he flushed with disgust to know she could be so easily and flaccidly pleased.

'Here,' she said, passing him a cushion and sinking onto the rag carpet. His long limbs folded down into themselves and he sat near her, not touching her.

'We have no future,' said Jain matter-of-factly, and Michael thought with a shudder that she sounded positively ecstatic. 'We could be extinct as a species in thirty years. That's a real possibility. We've done that to the planet and everything living on it, and we keep flying our planes and eating meat and making piles of rubbish and pretending it's all grand. Even if we don't all die, it's still going to be bad. It's going to be horrible.'

'What's the point of anything then?' Michael said. He was surprised by how sharp his voice was.

Jain looked surprised too.

'I ... I don't know.'

'Why are you making your art then?' he went on. 'What's the point of that? Who's ever going to see it?'

'I make it for me,' she said in a small voice. 'Because I have to.'

Michael didn't answer. He understood that she wasn't afraid, not truly afraid. It was still theoretical to her. She was trying to impress him, appeal to him, and this disgusted him – the lengths she'd gone to with the diorama, and how she'd still fallen short, even with her eyes shining. One look at her and you knew she wasn't a person who'd ever lain awake at night and felt the floor next to her bed open up into a vast and depthless yawn. No one Jain knew well had ever died. She was so pretty and petite; the void just didn't suit her.

For a second time, he realised she wasn't going to speak and so he had to. She was looking at him as if he'd just clapped in her face, her mouth slightly open and her eyebrows drawn together.

'I like your socks,' Michael said finally. Jain's socks had little strawberries on them. She didn't answer, but moved her foot closer so he could see them better.

'Chinese people find feet very erotic,' Michael said. 'They used to bind them up all small and deformed, but they were into that.'

Jain let a few seconds pass, and then said her sister once went on a date with a foot fetishist. They laughed tentatively about foot fetishists.

'Your one would be after your feet,' Michael said.

Jain flexed them experimentally.

'Have I got nice feet?'

'You've got nice everything.'

'What's everything?'

'Your hair,' Michael said, his heart pounding.

'What else?'

'Your neck.'

'My neck?'

'Yes.'

'What else?'

'Your wrists and your long fingers.'

'These fingers?'

'Yes.'

'What else?'

'Everything —' Michael was blushing and in agony, '— I like everything.'

Then Jain leaned over and kissed him, and soon they were lengthwise over the cushions, Michael fumbling with the buttons of her incomprehensible vintage dress. But when she took him up into the loft bed and they undressed, his penis just lay small and floppy like a tube of pulp against his thighs, insensate to the urging of Jain's long fingers, her pert mouth. Worse, he felt himself shrivelling up when she touched him, and his anger returned, alongside an absurd desire to cry, to throw up, to push her out of the loft bed.

'It's okay,' Jain said, snuggling her head against his chest. 'It doesn't matter, it really doesn't. I like you a lot, Michael.'

And she kissed his chest three quick times to prove it.

In the morning, Michael behaved like a counterfeiter of bills trapped in a lift with a recently swindled shop-owner.

'Will you ring me when you get back to Galway?' Jain said in the doorframe, twisting her hands.

'Sure.'

Except he didn't ring her. He went home and slept. Over the course of the next week they periodically exchanged texts and calls. Michael said he was sick. Jain said she'd come to Galway and bring him soup. Michael didn't respond. Jain asked if he was feeling better. Michael hinted darkly that he was sick in more ways than one. Then he said it was a mistake for him to have got involved with her.

but i like you, texted Jain. *i want to help.*

no one can help me, Michael responded, a day later.

Jain: *why are you being so dramatic?*

No answer. Then, two weeks later: *hey jain, any craic?*

just working on my pieces. how's you?

grand. working too.

Sender: ladsitsmichael@yahoo.com

Recipient: anna_c_surrey@gmail.com

Date: 02/02/12

Dear Anna,

Are you well? Recently I found some of the articles you've written and they really caught my attention. I've been reading a lot about climate change lately. This may be a strange question, but I was wondering whether you yourself are optimistic about humanity's shared future?

Yours,

Michael

Sender: anna_c_surrey@gmail.com
Recipient: ladsitsmichael@yahoo.com
Date: 02/02/12

Dear Michael,

Just a quick note as I'm running out the door, but you ask a pertinent question and I wanted to make sure I address it. I would say that yes, I'm optimistic. Here's why: to save as much of the planet as we possibly can, we have to act now, and to effect that kind of change we must believe that the sacrifices we're making will work. I'm so glad you've taken an interest in climate science – if you have any more questions, don't hesitate to ask. I strongly encourage you to get involved with local initiatives; I'm enclosing some links.

All the best,

Anna

That was the last time Michael wrote to her.

In June, Michael officially took a leave of absence from college. His sister came over for a chat, leaving the baby at home with her husband. She fixed tea, sat down.

'Well, Michael,' she said. 'I don't have a clue what's been going on with you, but I think you're making a big mistake.'

Michael didn't respond. He had no intention of participating in any scene that would result in catharsis; the goal was simply to endure the next twenty minutes.

His sister sat bunched up, her hands curled around a teacup, her eyes boring into him and her tight curls resting like compacted springs on her shoulder. As soon as she moved her head, they'd bounce free.

'I think you're depressed,' she said. 'It's not normal, it's not grief.'

Michael responded with a half-laugh and the rubbing of his left eye.

'I don't really know what that means.'

'We can get you counselling you know. And maybe you should come stay with me and Eamon for a while.'

'Where would I sleep?'

'We'd figure it out, so.'

Michael concentrated on the still surface of his tea.

'I want to help you, Michael.' Now her hair bounced merrily, as if mocking the serious face she was making. He wanted to laugh. He'd nearly said something melodramatic – I'm beyond all help – but instead he shifted in his chair and sipped the tea.

'Can you give me something to go on at least?' his sister persisted. 'What kind of life do you want for yourself?'

'That's a stupid question.'

His sister looked up sharply. She had tender eyes; she was easily wounded.

'Please.'

'Maybe I'll go back to Amsterdam.'

'And what, work on the pub crawl again? I thought you hated it there.'

'It would be better than here.'

He watched her thinking, watched her as she decided to bribe him: just enough money to travel for six months, money only if he didn't drop out. His future, Michael felt, was like a film that looked to be shite, but which he was being forced to watch anyway. So when his sister made her offer, he shrugged and said grand.

III

Michael's sister sat him down on a Tuesday. That Thursday, an uncle who delivered kegs to London pubs called to say there was a job with him if Michael wanted it. The job had been dangled in front of him before, but no one, least of all the uncle, had taken the proposal seriously. But then Michael's sister said she thought it was a good idea, and where could Michael stay while he looked for his own gaff? 'With me,' said the uncle. 'Why not?' And so Michael took a laughably short flight across the Irish Sea, and was picked up at the airport by his uncle Dan, who was his mother's brother. They hadn't seen each other since the funeral.

'Michael, are ye well?' murmured Dan in the sprawling arrivals lobby, already turning like a weathervane towards the exit. A tall, hulking man with a rubbery-looking nose and a raspy voice, Dan rested one hand on Michael's shoulder. 'Out this way, me limo's out the back.'

'The limo' was Dan's delivery truck; he made that joke three more times on Michael's first day in London. Michael didn't mind. Dan didn't look at him with eyes gone all milky with concern. Dan was just asking to be liked, and if Michael obliged, life together would be peaceful and undemanding.

Work quickly restored a rhythm to Michael's days. For the first month he was unceasingly sore, though every morning when he got up he felt that little bit stronger. His young, gangly body took on bulk gamely, even as his uncle's beer gut retained its look of permanence. Michael began to resemble the edgy older brother of his former self. In the evenings, he and Dan would go for pints. Dan was known and liked in the pubs they went to, and soon so was Michael. He slept on Dan's sofa bed and felt no need to move out. Dan's girlfriend of six years had just left him. 'Did me a favour,' Dan grunted, and said no more. Michael mostly kept quiet too; they drank side by side and watched the football. After a while Michael started paying Dan a small rent, which mostly went on drink for the both of them.

When he had time off, Michael sometimes went to museums because they were free and he felt like he should. Once he stood at the foot of a gigantic Buddha for an hour, but mostly he strode forcefully through the rooms, barely glancing at the paintings. Other people drifted past him like fish in a tank; the guards sitting demurely by each exhibit stiffened when he passed, suspicious of his speed. He liked the Tate Modern best because the artists there were obviously taking the piss. There was one room that contained nothing but a diamond-encrusted skull, and he thought that was genius. He wondered if Jain knew about it.

Over the course of his acclimation to London, Michael kept spotting Anna in the distance. Or women like her. There was, he realised, an entire class of women like her: Annas from behind, Annas in profile, even invisible Annas he recognised by scent alone. She was a template, and so many of the women he watched on the tube, or who passed him in museums, would betray through the bridge of their noses, the slant of their eyes, the uptick of their mouths at the corners, some forgotten residue of Anna. Rationally he understood that London was too giant, that he could live there for a thousand years and never see her. He no longer really remembered what she looked like, and only saw her true face in dreams that recurred less and less. Once, an Anna-like woman emerging from a Spar had, two hours later, got on his bus and stood beside a seated woman who'd also reminded him of Anna. Observing the standing woman and the seated one, he could tell clearly that they didn't resemble each other at all. But still, there'd be times when he was riding an escalator up and he'd see a black-haired woman, slightly stout, riding the opposite escalator down, her head bent to the side, and his heart would stop. Worst was when he didn't see her anywhere, just felt her invisibly watching him, usurping the supernatural rights of his own dead mother.

He'd been sleeping badly for months when he started getting up early, before the sun, and going for walks. It was intoxicating to catch such a vast, peopled city as it lay grey and pink and barely stirring. Over time he began to see familiar streets transformed the way Jain had seen the interior of her Dublin house transformed, except for him it was grander; London pulsated vividly with corruption and he pictured it drowned beneath the sea; he saw the bleached plains of England on the horizon; he saw the mass graves and the skeletal gangs roaming through the wreckage of Oxford Circus, Hyde Park, the Cutty Sark.

One night Dan put his hand on Michael's shoulder as they stood waiting for the barman to acknowledge them.

'What's wrong wit ye?' said Dan.

'Nothing's wrong with me.'

The barman turned around and Michael shivered, Dan's hand dropping away. He saw death and failure inscribed in the lines of the barman's face. Decent but hardly bright, prone to repeating himself, this man was anything but a survivor. The muted TV behind him flashed images of flooded towns in Devon and

Cornwall. Michael turned away, clutching his pint, and for one searing moment he didn't know where he was.

He'd been living in London on Dan's sofa for six months, working hard, tossing back a succession of early evening pints, wrestling with the sheets half the night and traipsing back and forth across Camberwell at dawn when, finally, Michael did see her. Anna. It was three weeks till Christmas, the air flatly frigid. Dan had sent him to buy frozen pizzas from the newsagent just two blocks from the flat, and there she was. Swamped by a black bubbly coat carelessly unbelted, buying peanuts and cigarettes. Did she smoke before? He couldn't remember. He stood arrested in the aisle, staring like a wild animal fixed in place by the sound of a cocked gun, except no one was observing him – not the strung-out, misanthropic clerk, not the busted security camera, not the Pakistani mother with her toddler buying, kitchen roll, nor the drunk fondling cans, nor the two teenage boys, obviously high, and least of all, not Anna.

Nearly two years had passed since he shared the *anti-kraak* with her in Amsterdam. She was thinner, her face in profile sharper somehow, more refined. He took the blast of her full-on when she left and swept the whole of the shop with a look. She didn't recognise him.

Michael, still standing dumbly in the aisle, started and exited the store. The night, now a deep ornate blue, had absorbed her tracelessly, and panic rose like vapour from his gut. But then, far ahead, disappearing between two parked cars, Michael spotted Anna's unmistakeable shape, a plastic bag swinging from her left hand.

Michael sprung to life, following her along the perimeter of Lucas Gardens, all festooned with fairy lights. He'd identified so many Annas over his months in London that he fleetingly wondered if he might be making a mistake. But watching the woman up ahead, he knew there was no mistaking her. Her body in motion sung in a frequency he'd been tuning into for years. Even the glossy black coat, hinged open in that slovenly way, had such an Anna-ness to it. He could imagine how it reeked of her.

Now she was twenty metres ahead, the bag swinging back and forth, her gait rapid. It was the cold making her walk so fast. He kept his eyes fixed on her, terrified of losing her like a pin in the ocean of London. No one noticed: it was so cold, so dark, and the people shuffling on and off buses were interrogating the pavement, their bags, their phones.

Then Anna took a sharp left. She was heading in the opposite direction from where Dan lived, but Michael didn't hesitate. From his many early-morning walks, he could practically map all of Camberwell from memory. It was his territory. Anna's hair bounced free and haphazard against the bubbly coat; she switched the plastic bag to her right hand.

She hadn't once turned around. He could tell now from the way her head was bent that she was looking at her phone. He followed her up the street and then lost her briefly. He was running, wild, when he spotted an alleyway between a row of terraced houses and darted into it instinctively. The alleyway was poorly lit and dotted with flowerpots, some broken, some containing the remnants of dead and half-dead plants. He knelt amongst the shattered pottery and some insane, uncensored commentator in his mind chastised him for trampling an exhibit in the British Museum. The damp soil seeped through to his knees. He could see out where the alleyway opened onto a dead end, and finally where Anna, again switching the plastic bag to the opposite hand, wrangled in her coat pocket for keys and approached a mid-terrace house. He waited, his heart pounding, as she entered and shut the door with a noise like a shot. Some three minutes later a light went on in an upstairs room. He couldn't see her silhouette, but the light was enough. He watched the lighted window until he forgot where he was and why. Then his phone buzzed in his pocket and he fumbled for it, Dan's number dancing across the screen.

Suddenly Michael remembered the pizza errand; he had no idea how long he'd been gone. When he stood up stiffly he felt something brush against his hand and saw that it was a spider. He knocked it off in revulsion, but there was another one on his trouser leg, and then another. The flowerpots were overrun with spiders, and they had colonised him as he kneeled among them, spying on Anna. A fit of disgust broke over him, and he stamped about in the darkness, killing spiders and breaking more pots, until a light went on in a nearby house and he heard voices. Michael ran.

The next night, he returned to the alleyway and stood where it opened like an orifice onto the rounded street. It was nearly ten, and the upstairs bedroom light was on again. The evening after that, he waited for hours by the street where Anna had made the sharp turn, but she failed to appear. Undaunted, he came back the next day, and was rewarded when a bus emitted her fifteen minutes after he assumed his watch. She wore the black coat again, but it was belted this time, plus a scarf, knitted hat, and boots with a slight heel. He thought she must be coming from work. He put up his hood and held his breath as she passed him.

The next night he borrowed Dan's coat. He told Dan he was seeing a girl. He followed Anna through the alleyway, careful this time, serene in the knowledge that he couldn't and wouldn't lose her, that now he only had to remain unseen. In the weeks leading up to Christmas, Michael learned several important facts:

Firstly, Anna's housemates were an Indian couple and an older woman who wore a lot of makeup; they had similar hours to Anna, but she rarely went out with them. Secondly, few neighbours used the shortcut which was the alleyway, and there were only two windows that looked onto it: one, obscured by a floral curtain, seemed to belong to a kitchen, while the other was narrower and covered with blinds. Lastly, the alleyway was flanked by small storage sheds belonging to residents of the adjacent terrace houses, and one night, after watching Anna's light go on, he put on his gloves and started trying the handles of shed doors, until he found one weak enough to break.

Michael broke the shed door two days before Christmas. His sister had wanted him to come home, but he refused. She'd said icily, 'Well, keep Dan company so. You're two lost souls.' He and Dan defrosted a feast, got pissed in the kitchen, and then Dan made a jumbled, inchoate speech of affection for Michael, interspersed with insults so it wouldn't go to his head ('You're a good lad ... a waster, sure, when the kegs are shoulder-high ...'), and they laughed till they cried and then ate pie. On St Stephen's Day he checked the shed lock and it was exactly as he'd left it; the owners were likely away. Anna had disappeared the day before Christmas, but he was assuming she'd be back for New Year's. He knew from his weeks of watching that she liked a night out.

And when she went out, he thought, swallowing another bite of pie, he would tell Dan he was seeing his girl, and then he'd go to the alleyway and watch Anna leave. She'd have lipstick and heels on and she'd look pretty and excited, indistinguishable from the other Annas similarly attired all over the city. No one she met out that night would know that she was the original one, with an evil design in her like an infected organ most people didn't see.

Dan stood at the top of the stairs as Michael paused by the door, pulling on his trainers.

'Well,' said Dan.

Michael dropped his keys into the pocket of his coat.

'I'm off. Happy New Year.'

'Happy New Year,' repeated Dan, and then he made a noise in his throat like he hoped to go on. With his hands in his pockets, Michael waited, looking up.

'Does she understand you, lad?'

The blood drained from Michael's face as he and Dan locked eyes.

'Well ...' said Dan again, but Michael cut him off, speaking rapidly to his shoes.

'I'd say she does.'

'All right,' said Dan. 'Take care of yourself.'

Michael fled, accidentally slamming the door behind him. The icy, black-and-blue streets of Camberwell had never looked as gorgeous as they did just then.

At 3:52 that morning, Anna stumbled home greasy-faced and radiant from the only free Tube ride Londoners get all year, and Michael stopped her in the alleyway by the broken shards of pottery. He'd been confident that he could stop her, he was strong enough now, and he wasn't wrong in this. First he gagged her and then he frogmarched her into the shed, where he'd already cleared a space. Her hair was rough and fragrant, and her heart beat like a fat moth against his forearm as she moaned faintly. Back in the flat, Dan's head lolled against the sole armchair and the sitting room was quiet but for the sound of traffic outside. Anna, her black eyes blinking furiously in the blackness of the shed, wasn't able to say anything, but Michael had prepared a speech.

Sheila Armstrong

Sheila Armstrong grew up in the west of Ireland and now works as a freelance editor. She has been shortlisted twice for the Over the Edge New Writer of the Year and once for the Words on the Waves Fiction Award. She was a runner-up in the Dromineer Literary Festival Flash Fiction Award 2014, and a nominee in the First Fiction category of the 2015 Hennessy Awards. She has been published in *Icarus*, *The South Circular*, *Literary Orphans*, the *Irish Independent*, *Litro* magazine and *gorse*.

The Tender Mercies of its Peoples

I

The smell in the bathroom of the intercity train is thick; layers of vapours piling up into a fetid moussaka that makes every trip to the bathroom an exercise in endurance. The stench seeps out from underneath the door, finding miniscule gaps in rubber seals and penetrating down the carriage. An automated voice warns to lock the door to ensure privacy, but there can be no privacy here, behind the curved and sliding grey door. Bodies have been here; bodies that once turned slowly in a red-tinted womb, that spouted first words with equal fervency, that learned not to fill nappies instinctively with wet and that defecation is a private, shameful thing. And then, years and months and days later, these bodies have been forced to share this space, this plastic cubicle that moves and jerks and rattles, this place where no surface is constant, and so they had left pieces of themselves behind, to endure.

From above, the body of the train seems to billow as the sky lightens and darkens, lightens and darkens, scaling its green skin and turning its usual grunting movement into a delight of

161

stop-motion animation. As the train track draws closer to the capital, other lines appear and wriggle sycophantically alongside it – rivers, roads, other railways, all converging in a giddy, draining movement eastwards, always eastwards.

After a ten-minute delay at one of the few remaining level crossings just outside the city, the train slides into the main station and coasts to a halt at platform three. One door opens a microsecond before the others and a foot squeezes out, followed by a torso, and another foot, and a whole person. Then more come; two and four and sixteen and the crowd continues to increase exponentially and there will soon be no room in between people to move, to sneeze, no space to be, no cracks for air to drift through, only sweaty armpits and umbrella spikes at eye level and suitcases with wheels that can't spin. And still they come.

But the flow peaks eventually and then slides back down into a slow drip, until all that is left on the platform is a tired Slovakian woman trying to manoeuvre the trolley down a too-narrow ramp. She feels the imagined itch that comes from a day of handling coins passed to her from countless human hands, and after her shift, she plans to run her arms under the hot tap all the way up to the elbow until the water sears her skin.

As the trolley jerks off the ramp and onto the level platform surface, two sugar packets are jarred loose and fall down, down, onto the tracks.

II

Down the street and around the corner from the train station, two large blue doors sit under an arch of red stone. Above them, the words 'Coroner's Court' are embellished in golden letters. To the side of these doors, a six-foot-high sheet of metal acts as a gate. The entrance that it blocks is wide, even bloated, and it is also painted a cheerful royal-blue. More blue fencing slides away down the street and pools in sticky puddles at the corner of the scene. The tops of the fences are jagged, carved into little troughs and peaks that create a new and more cut-throat horizon. There is No Parking here.

The building itself creates a sloping indentation in the street, a rock on a taut white sheet, and yet this depression is only visible from a single, unique perspective, the perspective that draws people to this area in the first place. The closer to the building, the greater the distortion, and passers-by instinctively speed up as they draw closer, trying to build up enough momentum to allow them to escape the gravitational pull of this structure.

A woman approaches the building, having left the train station on foot. She has a small wheelie bag, and one of the wheels is dented so that it traces a wobbling S-shaped path along the concrete. The train timetables are awkward; eleven o'clock is the allotted time, and the train has just pulled into the station at ten past ten. She considers taking some time to rest. Perhaps to sit somewhere and nurse a cup of peppermint tea. Order a hard-boiled egg and some toast, even. It might prepare her, give her strength. Because she shouldn't have come alone, they said, they all told her not to come at all. But this is not something she will accept, and the cold, clinical attraction of boxes waiting to be ticked and papers signed draws her like a lodestone.

So instead of waiting until the scheduled time, she walks directly down the street from the train station, around the corner, and along to the two blue doors. Her bag bounces and chafes along the uneven footpath, creating a waspish buzzing that annoys both her and those passing. As she approaches the red-stone building, she does not slow to compose herself, nor does she worry about arriving too early. She does not check her sleeves for a hurriedly secreted wad of toilet paper in case of tears. She does not ask God to give her strength, does not cast her eyes upwards in supplication. She does not do any of the things she feels she is expected to do, and of that she is proud. But she does pause as she reaches the blue doors, puts out an arm to force them open, and gives an extra tug on her suitcase to chivvy it along.

It is mid morning, and September, but the sun is still strong. The glare makes it difficult to see inside, but she disappears into the darkened maw of the building and the doors come together slowly behind her, softened by a spring that makes their slow movement a solemn genuflection. Their pace slows further as they draw closer together, until the last few centimetres are devoured and the line between inside and out is firmly sketched out once more. And then they are closed.

III

All around, the buildings wave like cilia, rows of protuberances that sway in tandem and filter the dirt and germs out of the air; trapping the impurities and enclosing them before they drift down to street level. The street is speckled with glass and iron and plastic, but the red-bricked building pulls at them and the walls eventually bleed into each other until the colours settle at a neutral wavelength.

Down the street, just a handful of steps away, there is an alley, a narrow cobbled walkway protected by a curving bridge painted in yellow and black. The dark walls are pebbled, and are painted with little pockets of words that press outwards and shove against each other, swelling and softening and merging.

An elderly man has found a groove tight enough to prop his spine against. He is asleep and snoring, a golluping sound as he

164

inhales, followed by a pause – so long a listener would be sure life had expired – and then a hoofing, whorling splutter that whines itself away down the alley. The man's beard is grey, curling slightly to one side, as if in response to the sun that creeps in at the east end each morning. Wiry and stiff, the beard seems an entity in itself, not one made of a thousand whispering grey hairs. He wears a red Fruit of the Loom fleece that dates back to the days before the company went under, spilling jobs like a discarded bag of apple-drops. His shoes are heavy work boots, with crenelated beige soles, and he has neatly stacked four cans of cider and a notebook filled with words in the nook behind his bent knees.

He has problems with his bladder, he will tell you, if you ask. When he wakes up each morning he mustn't move too quickly, or the accumulated waste of the night will spill out and ruin his only pair of underwear. It has happened before, and he is a cautious man. Coughing, raising his arms or sitting up too quickly will cause the flow to begin, and once it has started no clenching of pelvic muscles or act of supreme willpower can stop it. If he does manage to rise up slowly, so slowly, and get to the opposite wall in time, the piss that splashes into the drainage grate is brown and orange like rotting pumpkins.

Further into the alley there is a man with staring eyes. He has one shoe on; the other foot is bare, skeletal and pockmarked. The bones in his face strain as if trying to escape. In his hand he holds a single-use needle, a hard edge in a place of curves, of flabby air pockets. Slowly, so slowly, he brings it up to his face. His eyes flicker, but languidly, as if his pupils have been dipped in treacle and rolled through flour. The needle finds his left eye, hesitates for a moment over the white filmy surface, and then descends. There is an audible pop, and the air leaks out in a steady stream, deflating first the eyeball, then the left side of the skull indents itself, the cheekbone retracts, the jaw clenches upwards towards the new hole, and the neck puddles around the shoulders. The breastbone falls inward until it hits the spine, arms flap uselessly and the pelvis hits the tarmac with a slight chink-chink sound. It rolls, in a jolting, elliptical movement, picking up momentum as it goes – because the road here is slanted towards the gutters, so that rainwater and rubbish will slither towards the drains – until it comes to a rest against a rusted iron grate.

And then, all in one motion, he reinflates, and is whole again.

IV

The sun moves across the sky, pulling hours down like old paisley curtains torn from a bay window. The blue gates of the coroner's court remain shut, but a window in the building creaks open so someone can look at the clouds billowing in overhead and tut-tut-tut. It closes again.

At lunchtime the street begins to fill with people. They dribble along the footpaths and buy sandwiches with coleslaw and lettuce and chicken fillets, no mayonnaise. Then the street empties again, and the clouds begin to thicken further, and it is not long before an army of tight and plump raindrops begins to hammer down on the street.

V

'Cunt.'

Feet thump along the pavement. A woman is jogging past the building with the two blue doors. It is not the sprightly, clean, determined gait of an experienced runner; her face is red and her belly hangs down over her pair of forty-euro sports leggings; water-resistant, extra support, breathable fabric. The rain is falling harder now, and each step sinks a few inches into the concrete before bouncing back out, leaving grey reverberations that ripple outwards until they either hit the blue fence or drop lazily off the pavement and into the gutter below.

The woman gets out early from the office on a Tuesday, and so she forces herself into her white runners and out the door again before she loses momentum. It is an odd route for her to take – through the centre of town, along by the train station, around the corner past the coroner's court, before looping back up the hill – but she feels that the hundreds of eyes on her backside will encourage some shameful perseverance, and so she soldiers on.

But every evening, the man is there. Not every evening, of course, but most evenings, or some evenings; enough, at least, for her to mark the frequency of it happening and write it down in scratches on her skin. Dark-haired and well-dressed, he waits just off the corner of the square that sits clingingly close to the blue railings that surround the coroner's court. Sometimes he leans against a black iron bollard with a swelling on top that truncates in a black and oily pustule. Other times he is sitting on a bench with a sandwich wrapper between his knees and a briefcase at his feet, as if he had just happened by. But she knows he has not; he has come for one purpose only.

'Cunt.'

If the word were aimed directly at her, perhaps accompanied by the raising of a fist or the voice, it would be better. If he would call a little louder she would shout back or give him the finger. If he would look lecherously towards her ankles, tracing them in wide orbits with his eyes before aiming his sights higher, up her grey leggings, and further; if he would lick his lips and perhaps make groping movements towards her breasts it would be easier. She would shout at him then, or maybe attack him. She thought of her keys wound around her fist and the long, jagged edge of her bike key protruding between her index and middle finger. She would slash, first, if he stepped towards her, bending her knees into a half-crouch and rising onto the balls of her feet. He would roar and leap for her, and it all would descend into a mass of flailing limbs, of tearing skin, of ripped clothes and hanks of hair.

But he does not do any of these things – he mutters, as if talking to the air itself, and she cannot take enough offence to retaliate.

Instead, she jogs faster, and as she turns a corner he falls out of sight, and she tries to focus on her breathing. Now that she has passed the red-bricked building, with vision blurred by the rain, she finds her steps coming a little lighter. She speeds up, and jerks her head in a determined half-motion that signals a reaffirmation of will. And still the words reverberate in time with the pounding of her feet on the hard concrete.

Cunt. Cunt. Cunt.

The bass-laden music in her headphones is suddenly replaced by silence, and a text message interrupts the pounding soundtrack of her disgrace. She gasps in relief at the opportunity to slow and check her phone. It is her husband, and they are out of milk.

She walks the rest of the way home.

VI

Four o'clock, the daily exodus out of the city just beginning. A dog winds its way through legs and tartan trolleys, stopping to cock a leg against the blue gates. A female pit bull mix, bred for fighting, with ears that have been clipped close to the skull. The tail has been docked so as to offer less grip for an opponent, less loose skin that could be torn and bled. There is a ragged scar that reaches from under its jaw, dips to the belly, and fades before surfacing again in the groin. Because of this, it is missing two nipples, but what use has a dog for nipples?

It had been no good as a fighter, so they tied it up by the hind legs, with ropes that bit so deeply they left scars that would never heal, and allowed the other more crazed dogs free rein as a warm-up. Once, it had been kicked so hard in frustration that ribs crackled and the dog collapsed in a wheezing pile, spasming and vomiting all over itself. But the damn thing didn't have the decency to die, and when the first man had come back to the shed the next morning, it had dragged itself over to his feet and smiled a doggy smile that was so stupid and affable that the man found himself giving the dog some water, a blanket, and eventually delivering him as a present two weeks after his son's birthday. The mother was distraught, and the man had been chased off with no offer of tea, or a plate of food, or what he liked to call a tidy fuck – one that didn't involve removing his shoes or even his trousers all the way. But the dog was given rashers that were only two days out of date, and had smiled its dopey smile until it fell asleep.

The rain has stopped, now, outside the coroner's court, and the dog pauses in the doorway, considering. A few hands lower themselves and scratch the dog behind its ear stubs, but most passers-by step back automatically. An evolutionary trait, perhaps, one that had served some furry ancestor well as it huddled in a ditch while a four-legged predator slunk past. The ones that reach down to pat it are the ones that will end up savaged in their beds by feral beasts and left unnoticed for a week, abandoned to marinate and produce a foetor so strong that neighbours can no longer blame it on the drains, and will be forced to call a locksmith to open the door.

The pit bull mix waddles on, leaving behind a stream of urine that has coloured the doors a darker blue, and the building ripples slightly in the dog's wake.

VII

As the shadows stop lengthening and begin to meet in the centre of streets and join into a whole, the doors of the coroner's court finally reopen. They have opened before during the day; sometimes they have even been held open as clusters of twos and threes have passed through, but those openings have been muted, dull, compared to the sharpened and underlined opening that now occurs.

The woman steps out onto the pavement, and words and phrases bound around her, excited puppies tearing at her sleeves in an attempt to gain some attention. They roll under her feet, ecstatic, and she stumbles, throwing out her hands to break her fall. Her wheelie bag lurches, and one wheel flies a few centimetres into the air before crashing back down and swivelling crazily in a ninety-degree turn.

Some passers-by glance in her direction, but two have already stopped to help her to her feet. A man and an older woman are grasping her elbows, attempting to pull her up. She resists, fiercely — what arrogance, what presumption — and makes her body weigh as much as possible. She pours lead into her bones and lets it trickle down to her feet, where it pools, searing the pavement around her until it cools and hardens. With one fist to the ground and the other to her waist, and this heavy, rippling base of lead around her feet, she becomes a toy soldier, poised to move into action, to race towards enemy lines, to save the day.

And, with her head down, she sees that loss is a pit that becomes more cavernous and bottomless as the sides slope downwards. Further up, little ridges and crevices grow where a piton can be wedged to stop or at least delay the inexorable slide into the depths. And then, spilling out from the epicentre, where the slope begins to lessen and the slippage is not so noticeable; a falling body will come to a rest, eventually, but little furrows will build up in U-shapes around their stationary forms. And from then on out the way is smooth, except for certain humps and bumps and holes that people will find in their lives, when their thoughts drip down into the cavern below. Some people, like spelunkers, chain themselves to those who descend to the deepest parts. Not to make sure they can pull those sorry souls out, no, they hang on so that waves of reflected grief will wash over them and they will have some shared mortality and feel more human on account of the pain. She sees this and more, and more, and she sees destruction everywhere, the self-loathing that lies in every bitter and desiccated soul, and she cannot stop seeing, and it burns, and it hurts, and, and, and....

And then, after a lifetime, she turns her head, and the people holding her arms in confusion and wondering why she seems as heavy as a neutron star feel a great lessening of the weight and are able to pull her up. She smiles and thanks them and is embarrassed by her own clumsiness. No, she has not hurt herself. No, just a crack in the pavement, no dizziness, just a stumble. Thank you, and thank you, and yes, and thank you. The rogue suitcase is reclaimed, and the man and the older woman continue on their way, in opposite directions, both briefly enveloped in an altruistic smugness.

The woman has booked a hotel. There are a number in this area, and she had chosen the first one that had appeared in an internet search. There will be a bed there, and a bath, and perhaps a jar of gently scented flowers. A TV, a radio, a kettle. A mint on the pillow, because the owners are American and believe that this demonstrates the height of hospitality. A cream rug, freshly hoovered. White and blue embroidered sheets. Continental breakfast included; cooked food, extra. She can sleep, and recover, and spend time alone reflecting on the day.

It is the best option, and her other son will worry if she doesn't rest. She needs to rest, and rest, and rest, but the world will not rest alongside her, or pause to let her breathe, it will not stop and turn itself off for a second, just a second, a SECOND, to acknowledge that what was once there is gone.

So she leaves the blue gates under the red-bricked arch behind, turns the corner and walks back to the train station to catch the last train home.

VIII

The full train sits at rest in the station, muzzled and whining at the delay as the Slovakian woman manhandles the refilled trolley back onto the first carriage. She is low on packets of milk, but she has noticed that passengers on the evening trains usually order soft drinks rather than tea or coffee. At this time, too, she knows that the aisles will be packed with out-of-breath students, crouching on their hunkers or whispering in low, careful conversations. The trolley will not have space to move for at least an hour, until the excess flow trickles out and the contents of the train resettle themselves into the vacated seats. So she sits back and takes out her book, a glistening paperback with an unbroken spine.

A whistle blows, and a piercing beeping signals the departure of the train, and it pulls away slowly, unsure of itself. The smell of the toilets drifts out and into each adjoining carriage. They have been cleaned four times today, but the ammonia in human waste seems to form a weak acid that infiltrates all it touches at a molecular level. Parents cling to swaying children as they step over reclining bodies on the floor and into the cubicle, before screwing up their noses at the stench. When they leave, their child having performed, they wrinkle their noses again and shake their heads at the people outside, as if to signal that they had no part in the creation of that awful odour.

The train moves out of the city, for a time running alongside rivers and roads before they reluctantly depart and curve back around to their guarding duties. The train picks up speed and holds a steady course; a steel and timber axle around which the whole country turns. Only the canal is left to shepherd it along, and very soon it too goes its separate way.

It is full dark now, and the disappearing lights are a harsh jest against the still waters of the canal. Reeds drawn from childhood memory trace the canal edges, and a high stone wall hems it in. There is a dead pigeon in the water. It floats near the edge, brushing against a fan of weeds that have been teased into a complex knot. A healthy algal bloom surrounds it, penned in by the black, oily waters, creating some heraldic mockery; *sable, bordure vert, pigeon mort*. Its dark-grey feathers fan out and wave in a slow, oscillating motion that barely quickens when the breeze swoops low over the canal surface and pushes furrows of stagnant water forwards, past the weeds, around the slight bend, over the discarded election signs, until the ripples come up short against the next lock and heave themselves over the edge of the six-foot drop.

Oisín Fagan

Oisín Fagan (b. 1991) is from Co. Meath. He has been previously published in *The Stinging Fly* and *New Planet Cabaret*.

Subject

1

Heterosexual, Caucasian, sub-bourgeois, Irish, post-peasant, empowered, lonely, distant when sober, misogynist when drunk, loving when stoned, Irish, twenty-two, unemployable, somewhat educated, but nevertheless inadequate at synthesising and actualising education into any productive format, finds it difficult to imagine anything that is not slight variation on direct experience, never read a book, never will, competent in Word, Spreadsheet, Excel, can type forty words a minute, proficient in CPR, woodwork, welding and technical graphics, Leaving Certificate Applied, provisional driving licence, doesn't want to join the Guards, loved and/or lost, capable of making connections, but untrusting, and increasingly untrustworthy, tenuous hold on reality three hours a day (in the morning), assertive and enabling between midday and 9 p.m., incapable, guilt-stricken, takes communion once a month, struggles to believe in God, struggles to believe that the Catholic legacy should be destroyed (N.B. was sexually abused by teacher not priest, didn't tell anyone because didn't care, or did care but did not know what caring entailed, so young, little to no trauma incurred), takes MDMA once a month, smokes weed twice a month, but hates it, in reality the son of a small dairy farmer and

a secretary who works in a primary school, lost virginity at fifteen
to a schizophrenic drug dealer from Limerick (she said her name
was Amy, but it wasn't; she had a beautiful smile, but her eyes were
vacant, she did not know who she was, sometimes her mind would
draw a blank and a white abyss would spread before her like an
endless tapeworm, but even then she could dominate whoever she
met with the suggestion in her smile and the question mark that
hung inside her every word like a lung-trapped breath) who fell
pregnant at seventeen (not subject's child), virginity regained at
nineteen when subject fell in love with woman who fell in love with
him and would later provoke a two-year-long breakdown that subject is lucky to survive, hating, violent, though does not condone
violence, prone to month-long bouts of depression every three
months, never edges out of the depression like used to, hands
against the wall, no more extreme highs or deep-rooted beliefs,
quite intense lows, can't articulate pain, still cries when sees children, good relationship with mother, fair relationship with father,
bad brother to four sisters, lonely, but unwilling to compromise
solitude, dreams of sex-slaves and then punches self full in the face
when realises what he has become one hot morning in August,
promptly masturbates, emigrates to Los Angeles with money from
working summer in sawmill, gets raped (again), this time in South
Central Los Angeles by forty-year-old obese black man with gun,
when black man is finished sodomising subject, injects him with
syringe in left buttock, terror, accepts death, bothered by the heat,
sweats in dark rooms, covers himself in ice that melts in hot seeps
across torso, the fan is broken and the air is dead, finds out HIV
negative and feels strange affinity with black obese forty-year-old
for provoking burst of life, rape as a form of invigoration, thankful
to be alive all summer but still afraid of love, still incapable of said
love, tries to deal weed, but fails miserably as gives most of it away

for free and can no longer smoke it because the terror at this stage
is constant, books tickets home online when drunk, somehow
finds a printer somewhere, wakes up, receipt for tickets across chest
next morning but has no memory of tickets or their booking so
sees it as divine sign, goes back to Granard, Longford, and detoxes
by gardening for local millionaire, millionaire then goes bankrupt
because of planning permission fuck-up, but probably because of
capitalism and/or insider-trading plus cronyism, does youth work
and realises starving illiterate children have more control over their
own emotions than he does, there is no money in youth work and
state penalises it, dole gets cut, finds no happiness in miniscule
progress children make, but does find ideal woman who will not
allow subject to fall in love with her, woman works in Centra and
spends evenings playing with her little sister and reading fashion
magazines though she wears only Nike, gynaecologically speaking
she is a new high for subject, woman tells subject to go home and
get a life and grow up and be a man, woman does this because she
is perfect and subject believes this because subject believes himself
to be chronically imperfect, plants four trees in her garden in a
square formation as a parting gift (she allows this, this much she
will allow, but no more) and writes his initials into their young
bark and waits for the young bark to grow over them so he can be
effaced, promptly masturbates, can't sleep any more, unsure of
reality, too much solitude, for some reason feels need to go to
Buenos Aires (there is beauty there), but can't afford a ticket, dole
is cut (again), can't hold down a job because boredom is worse than
loneliness and there are no jobs for fuck-ups like subject, but also
there are no jobs period, so begins to workout and go for runs and
cuts down on cigarettes, meanwhile, subject's mother is going
insane with grief at the breakdown of her marriage but son (subject) doesn't notice, after three months subject has lost six kilos and

is tight as a drum so looks in the mirror, laughs, and that night begins eating curry chips every night for the next year and feels too lazy to do anything but watch Eastenders and Futurama and cry, decides must change life and realises is capable of appreciating beauty because there are so many beautiful moments everywhere and subject must understand them, then steps on loose nail in yard, goes right through the foot, realises this is like the injection and now at last might die, waits four days to go to doctor, but unfortunately no infection, no nothing, looks at pictures of London online and watches three Ken Loach films and decides that if he goes to England he will be dead from sadness within three months, woman he fell in love with at nineteen still visits him once a month and they fuck and cry for hours even though she has boyfriend because no one has a connection as pure as they do or can ever have a connection as pure as they do, it's not infidelity she says, it's a deeper truth, starts working in Tesco, by this stage is masturbating five to eight times a day with the aid of newly introduced broadband, promptly masturbates, house prices are rising dramatically but this does not affect subject, as long as subject is in Ireland there is no threat of subject leaving childhood bedroom, due to broadband a year goes by lost to near-constant masturbation, helps father on farm, but can't stomach violence of cutting haunches any more, decides he has no friends (they are all in Australia, England, Canada, nobody goes to America any more, except for students on J1s and assholes, though there is some crossover) and joins dating website and when takes selfie realises he is twenty-five, fat, balding, unskilled and underfucked, starts working out again, tries to write how he is feeling and ends up with one sentence that has no verb and can't think of anything, then writes that down, no friends, Granard isn't working out, back in childhood bedroom, pulls out box from under bed, looks at his Mé Féin essays and realises that when he was a child he thought things would happen when he grew up but they never did, and he never imagined he would be fat and he is still getting fat, but subject is quite happy that more women than he expected are attracted to baldness as long as you keep the sides close-cut, otherwise it's embarrassing, realises emigration is only choice, mother cries at Dublin Airport gate as subject waves goodbye (she drove him down because he cannot afford car, driving lessons, insurance, petrol, N.C.T. etc. Same. Old. Shit.), she cries but she knows he will fail abroad and come back, which makes her happy as all her four daughters have emigrated though the two eldest daughters are in Dublin and come home every second weekend but she still counts it as emigration and feels guilty at how selfish she is, but she loves her son though he knows he doesn't deserve her love and realises that it's not really about deserving, it just is, and that's how they've survived so long, re-arrives in U.S.A., this time in New York City and immediately starts mixing cement for two scoundrels, one Irish, one who pretends to be Irish, Maloney O'Houlihan he calls himself, embarrassingly, three months go by and does not get raped again as is no longer attractive, feels slightly sad at this, realises that he will be unattractive forever, accepts it over the course of an hour and then takes half a gram of cocaine and spends all his money on three prostitutes who bite his testicles (only one of the bites is sensual and erotic, the others are aggressive, hungry and, frankly, hateful) and steal his wallet (which was empty, subject feels like he is the winner in this situation for some reason), still chronically underfucked, promptly masturbates, doesn't like sports for some strange evolutionary reason so can't talk to anyone about anything anywhere, to rectify this friendless situation promptly puts three weeks' wages on horse that's running in Grand National in the Old(er) Country, co-workers just think subject is mentally retarded and/or suffering breakdown, does not make friends and horse breaks its leg after scuffing the first jump and is put down on course but off camera, though now fat and bald never lets beauty-standard-subject-expects-of-women drop, which would involve assessment of current subject position in such a way that would require retroactive reassessment and realignment of past self-worth, which would eventually entail not only admitting current worthlessness, but would also entail an introspection of which subject is currently incapable, so remains underfucked, all meaning is leeched from this country, decides to work harder, no effect, no promotion, no nothing, still nine dollars an hour, still living eight to a room, three Irish, one German (woman, heroin addict) and four Puerto Ricans who all think subject is gay and look at subject strangely before they go to sleep on their respective pallets, calls mother late at night and does not ask her how she is doing, but tells her how he is suffering, sees chrysanthemums bloom one day on fourth avenue, on a windowsill, a high windowsill, as black men with their trousers low hover around wondering what fat bald pale Irish man is doing crying like a bitch at midday in the hottest summer in recorded history, these chrysanthemums send subject into nervous fits and subject realises subject is a bad son, calls mother and tells her how much he loves her, gives an accurate diagnosis of self to her and says that nothing will compromise that even though subject is shit at everything, including recognising that subject is shit, subject also realises that subject is shit to everyone else who accidentally loves subject, and even though subject recognises this subject swears that subject loves mother, this will be greatest moment of mother's life, mother who has made eternal constant sacrifices for nothing, nothing has ever worked for her, but son acknowledges that sacrifice, which is beautiful, on one level at least, she doesn't even mind that the call comes through at four in the morning (so beautiful how the light hits the trees in Granard, on Market Street, where subject's mother lives now subject's mother and subject's father are separated, which up till now has had minimal effect on subject), are you all right, my love? she asks her son, no, subject says, and smiles and cries and drinks his own tears, yummy, crying that at last he has said something that is a thing, a real thing, after two and a half decades of surly incomprehensible culchie stony-faced non-speak, strong, silent type gibberish made up of grunts and allusions and darkness and oneness, big breakthrough, rural weirdness is constant and never-ending, so much solitude, trapped in skull, trapped in back roads with unbroken strips of grass running down the centre for miles and miles, but actually still in New York City, later that week is shocked that everyone, everyone being all strangers to him, hasn't noticed big breakthrough, but soul is strong, it is, mother is appreciated, goes to a club and gets ignored, goes to work and gets ignored, goes home and ignores himself, arms are strong with work, strong and solid, but belly is expanding and taut with shit American Guinness, American women are far too attractive, even the white ones, but every now and again in clubs, when everyone is high, certain attractive women go blind, physically blind, with alcohol and other substances and can't see him, all they see are shimmering white and black spots, but they hear, and they hear subject's lovely soft, dulcet accent only slightly corrupted by all the violent American films he grew up watching, and then the beautiful women allow subject to sleep with them, this actually only happens once and subject fails to remember it he was so drunk, subject is drifting now, it is difficult to breathe here, the city is too humid and too hot and too everything and it is embarrassing how uncosmopolitan subject is, though given how many programmes subject has watched about cosmopolitan people it is not only embarrassing but astounding, subject may be drifting but is not incredibly unhappy, unreality exists on a certain plane of vision and experience so unhappiness is pleasantly obfuscated and replaced with something much weirder, closer to anxiety in its nature, but not anxiety, more like a tense numbness that is pink-tinged with insights of beauty, but mainly numbness, slips into a pleasant alcoholism and becomes fearless in regards to prostitutes, i.e. will fuck them and tip them and will not wear a condom, ambition, though there was never much, disappears and subject realises being a functional alcoholic is best option given state of affairs, no reason to say no to constant low-wave pleasure, fuck the future, it doesn't exist, and if it does it does not exist for us and it does not belong to us, nothing else is happening, smartest thing to do, this lasts for four months, a fine four months, feels proud to be an Irish illegal immigrant, a link in the chain of great illustrious forefathers, contracts herpes, which isn't too bad with all the lotions that are available on the market, and then when horrifically inebriated, so inebriated none of the senses work, not-a-one, calls former love of life in a cabin from a twenty-four-hour internet café on 109th Street and this ruins everything, everything, former love of life is pregnant, you have no right, subject says, that should be my child, subject says, former love of life lays some heavy truth on subject and says firstly subject never liked anyone but himself, I never liked myself, subject says, interrupting, don't interrupt me, former love of life says, secondly, in all likelihood subject probably hates women and/or thirdly, no connection is possible with such a terminally oblivious fuck-up, fourthly, you left me because you just couldn't handle reality, motherfucker, fifthly, hold on, wait a second, subject says, pouring heart out, I don't get anyone, and I don't care about men either, it's not just women, the rest is true, you admit that, former love of life says (she will always be the love of his life), and you admit all the rest, I do, subject blathers and sweats and feels like heart is stopping and subject will never drink again, subject swears to self silently, time to grow up, subject, always-love-of-life says, and always-love-of-life hangs up, subject looks at wall, promptly masturbates, leaves internet café in disgrace, semi-erect member hanging out of soiled O'Neill's shorts (Longford colours, not a big seller), Nigerian manager almost cries and wishes he had papers so could purchase a gun and shoot subject in head, cue intermission, signalled by a

2

Life is full of little insights that may add up to some nebulous definable point in the near future if subject is lucky, but in all likelihood they will not, and subject is now completely aware of surroundings and self, and can now frequently discern where the two intersect and where the two diverge, so bides time for opportunity to become full human being and achieve full human being status, subject knows this will happen, but not in America, which subject thinks is shit by the way, so bides time for two years, bides time to become a man, to use gendered term, but what subject means is human being, a fully operational one, that can do stuff, and not be shit all the time, subject wakes up every morning (there are now only Puerto Ricans in the flat, all the other Irish have moved on up in the world because they are white and speak English (these traits have not helped subject), and German woman is dead from overdose, all have been replaced by yet more Puerto Ricans who look like replicas of original Puerto Ricans, subject thinks in most uncosmopolitan way), and thinks about opportunity, and God give me the strength to recognise it if it comes, said opportunity must take into account subject's enormous capacity to fuck up everything all the time, but subject realises for most people opportunity never comes, then after one whole motherfucking year mother calls and says father is terminally ill and subject as only son must assume the mantle and cut the haunches, come home, dear, she pleads, subject almost cries with happiness at having responsibility, responsibility which hints at redemption, redemption from what?, why from nothing of course, of course mammy, poor daddy, just wire me the money to come home, what? cries mother, think about what you're saying for a moment and we on private insurance, those motherfuckers, oh shit, so subject works for three more months, saving every penny, must protect mother, no more drink, no more drugs, thins rapidly, halves himself in weight, cuts remaining hair, straggly hair that sprouts sideways out of head in uneven clumps, and cuts overgrown toenails frequently now, showers every day, stares at ceiling a lot and smiles every now and again, and then books tickets and smiles, and goes home after tipping Polish prostitute $200 and staining her nipples with tears and lines of MDMA, bye Puerto Ricans, you guys were all right, though you undercut all my brothers at every turn with your hard work and work for nothing, goodbye comrades, three years in the Biggish Apple and Irish skies are so grey that subject immediately falls into depression, which subject immediately pulls himself out of because for once subject is not the most important person in subject's life, goes home and the work starts immediately, mother has quit job as secretary, there is no income only outflows, mother does paperwork and has moved back in with father to care for him, the division of labour is that subject farms and mother wipes formerly estranged husband's arse and holds back father's hair while his chemotherapy calls for him to vomit into the sink or out the back door in the yard or any fucking place there is so little time once the worst nausea in the world hits you, and mother administers infinite pills into his bleeding mouth, my daddy is dying, subject realises, and turns to mother who has never stopped crying and who has never stopped caring for whatever she was allowed to care for, says to her, we're the team, us against the world, subject nods, finally someone I trust, mother smiles though she doesn't say this, assume the mantle, cut the haunches, subject gets up at six every morning to do the milking, comes back at midday to eat dinner in the kitchen, mother makes small talk, frowning father domineers in silence like a large shadow thrown on a wall, his scowl is constant, nobody has ever really known who or what he was, he has always just spilled hatred, his hatred used to flow out of him, now his hatred is turned inwards and is subdued and finite, subject eats dinner, drinks two pots of tea with Custard Creams, then subject lies down on couch and subject and mother watch daytime quiz shows, which she is very good at, or they play dominoes or twenty-fives, usually father remains at kitchen table in silence and anger at the world but mainly at his own body for no longer being under the sway of his indefatigable will, subject falls asleep, then at two o'clock goes out and works till six or seven, but time is irrelevant here, in all honesty life is not too bad, mother is happier, father could never be touched or moved so fuck him, but mother is happier, she starts praying and goes to Mass a lot, subject stands in the yard and hears the calves lowing and looks at the grey sky that tries to smother him and his boots are caked in dung and he thinks while I am not happy I am where I belong, and then starts moving bales of hay with a pitchfork and feels proud of himself and his father and his grandfather and all the tonnes of hay, the fields of hay, the oceans of ever-regenerating hay they must have moved over the centuries, subject goes out on a Friday night, but the only people vaguely caught up in his generation are the wrong side of it, still in school, sixteen, seventeen, eighteen, and he feels too guilty to fuck them, most of the time, few pints, goes home and watches box sets of The Sopranos or The Wire or Breaking Bad, but there is never enough quality TV to guarantee frequent bouts of low-level happiness, and wakes up at midday on Sunday and farms for ten hours a day, therapeutic happy work except for castration, market day, cutting the haunches, rarely thinks of rape now, slowly begins to find out where all the people he went to school with are, New Zealand mainly, but one is in Thailand, which sounds interesting, six months' hard graft, has meaningful conversations with mother about sisters three or four times a week, squeezes her hand before he goes to bed, father is getting thinner, looks like a rag doll, but lo and behold temporary remission, so a year or two at least, is life such a terrible thing to leave behind? yes, his soul says, and his mother nods, never leave life, no matter how limited, even in the limits there is enough glory for the ages, in the fields in the smiles in my family who I will never leave again, though he never says this and they never have this conversation and no one ever says anything like this ever though he can feel it in his soul, sometimes, for the craic he and mother start planning big Christmas get all the family back, looking at cookbooks deciding between goose and turkey, between cranberry and apple, between silver decorations and gold decorations, and then on Tuesday subject comes in from the yard at midday and the house is cold, which is strange, and he calls for his mother a few times then wanders around the house idly for a while, he sees his mother is dead on the pull-out couch beneath the sheets and he can hear his father is pottering around upstairs, slowly oh so slowly, and his heart dies and his eyes go vacant and he sits down next to her and kisses her cheek, which is revolting and cold and waxy, and he doesn't know why he does it, and he says oh no oh please no please no I can't, I just can't, and then he closes her eyes and realises he must and he takes off his wellies and his overalls and cleans his hands and then goes upstairs in a numb daze and administers IV to his father.